To Geoff

the park Keeper

Cecils friend

Best Wishes

Victoria Badda

On You Go

by
Victoria G. Baddon

Grosvenor House
Publishing Limited

The right of Victoria G. Baddon to be identified as the author of this
work has been asserted in accordance with Section 78
of the Copyright, Designs and Patents Act 1988

The book cover is copyright to Victoria G. Baddon

This book is published by
Grosvenor House Publishing Ltd
Link House
140 The Broadway, Tolworth, Surrey, KT6 7HT.
www.grosvenorhousepublishing.co.uk

This book is a work of fiction. Any resemblance to
people or events, past or present, is purely coincidental.

A CIP record for this book
is available from the British Library

ISBN 978-1-83975-697-9

Acknowledgement

Grateful thanks to Emma Joy for her encouragement and creative editing, making sense of my scrawling sentences.

For my mother, Joyce, who taught me the joy of freedom.

"On You Go"

By Victoria G. Baddon

The girl woke with a start and couldn't remember where she was. The room was dark and she could feel an arm over her body. She suddenly remembered the last-minute party she had gone to and that everyone had gone back to someone's house. She felt her head ache and her throat felt so dry; she wondered what time it was, and… who the arm belonged to! Carefully, she pushed the arm away and stealthily crept out of bed so as not to wake its owner, she quickly found her clothes and dressed. As she opened the bedroom door to leave, she glanced back at the sleeping figure and recognised the dark face on the pillow. She smiled as she left the room. Back at her student accommodation, she quickly showered and dressed and went into the kitchen to grab some breakfast. Her flatmate, Lucy looked up in surprise and said, "I didn't hear you come back last night, it must have been a good party" The girl replied "I think it was!"

CHAPTER ONE

Veronica walked briskly down the university corridor feeling happy she'd just left a room full of Business Study students with plenty to think about on a lecture addressing 'How to find business opportunities in unusual places,' which she'd initially been quite nervous about when the university had approached her for her input but was surprised how much she had enjoyed the students' interest and their quick-fire questions on so many different fronts. Before she entered the room, she took a deep breath and could hear Samuel's voice in her ear saying "On you go" just as he had done over the years when she was finding life difficult.

Now she was on her way to meet Georgina for lunch in Times restaurant. She had thought of all the occasions they had shared growing up together, even though Georgina was her cousin, she thought of her more as a sister. Georgina's mother, Rosie had brought them both up and they had a lovely childhood. Georgina had always been a bit of a tomboy, preferring to climb trees and play with her catapult while Veronica played with her dolls house. Georgina had her name shortened to George quite often, which she liked.

Veronica was a little early, so she ordered a glass of wine while she waited. She looked around the familiar restaurant she had visited so many times over the years. It combined beautiful, antique furnishings which included a marvellous grandfather clock and wonderful wall coverings with soft lighting which made it feel more like someone's living room than a restaurant. It was all very relaxing and she could have happily sat there on her own for hours.

Robin had seen Veronica stride in through the restaurant door from the reflection in the mirror. "Blast!" he thought, "It's lucky I'm tucked away around the corner at my usual table. That's a bore, I'll have to go out through the side entrance - good job I haven't ordered yet". He quickly got to his feet and stepped out into the street just as the waitress arrived to take his order. She sighed and went back to the bar and said, "Looks as though table four's had an urgent appointment." Robin quickly dialled the number and re-arranged his lunch date thinking that was a close shave as he didn't want Veronica tittle-tackling. He wondered if she was meeting up with Georgina.

Georgina arrived breathlessly as she was a little late and hugged Veronica. Looking well turned out as always and wearing her usual 'L Air Du Temps' perfume, she had very fair, long hair which fell just

2

below her shoulders and had a very attractive, intelligent face. She had a very busy life as a teacher at the local junior school as well as being a wife and mother and being a member of so many different clubs and causes, that Veronica had lost count. As she sat down, Georgina asked Veronica how her lecture had gone and listened with interest at all the questions she had been bombarded with and was relieved to see how much Veronica had enjoyed the experience, knowing that she'd nearly backed out because she was so nervous.

Georgina often reflected how different their lives had turned out. Veronica worked on one project after another, never staying with one long, before moving on to the next one and happy to live alone, but Georgina would have been happy to see her settled with someone. She felt her own life was like a juggling act of keeping her husband and daughter happy and trying to fit everything into the school curriculum.

Veronica asked Georgina how things were at school and she told her about the different projects and she was having trouble with one child in her class called Billy. He'd come from a troubled family and caused mayhem in the classroom. She'd tried all sorts to help him but was running out of ideas. Her friend Judith who worked with her at the same school had had many ordeals with him too, so they were trying to get their heads together to work something out to settle him down.

Veronica thought Georgina looked tired and asked if she was sleeping and Georgina went on to tell her how worried she was about her husband, Robin's behaviour and how she saw so little of him and that he seemed so far away. Veronica tried to reassure her and said, "Maybe he's having a tough time at work, he's never enjoyed working there, you've said many times", she sighed and said "Oh look our food's here, let's just enjoy our lunch". They raised their glasses up, clinked, and said "Cheers" as they tucked in. Georgina had ordered a gluten free vegetarian lasagne with salad and Veronica had salmon with parsley sauce and vegetables. As always, they shared a mixed dessert dish, they couldn't decide, so they settled for the trio dish which included cheesecake, fresh fruit meringue and chocolate toffee brownie.

After lunch, feeling happy and full, they said their goodbyes and Georgina rushed back to school while Veronica headed back to her apartment. The apartment was Veronica's third home. She bought her first house, a small cottage which needed a complete refurbishment and she learned so much about home improvements from damp proofing to re-roofing and all the costs that went with it. She enjoyed the interior decoration though and was very pleased with the results of her work in her cosy cottage. She sold the cottage and from the profits she bought a larger house in which she did more or less the same plus added a very nice landscape on the gardens with a circular driveway. After selling on, she now had her apartment in Encliffe Park which she loved. There wasn't a garden, but she did have a private roof terrace which was lovely to sit out on and view the stars in the evening.

CHAPTER TWO

Veronica loved her apartment; it was in a quiet bohemian area near the university on Encliffe Park Avenue. It was part of a majestic Victorian building and the rooms were very light with large windows overlooking the park. The ceilings were very high with ornate coving and she had a period fireplace with a Victorian surround. She had furnished her living room with Persian rugs and tapestries which made the room look very warm and welcoming and had an Eastern touch about it. The walls were filled with a high bookcase which were crammed full of books on a diverse selection of topics.

Veronica threw her shoes off and had changed into comfy jeans when the voice through the intercom shouted "It's me gorgeous, are you accepting handsome strangers, or will I do? Laughing, she pressed the door open, recognising Samuel's magnetically charismatic Scottish baritones. Samuel walked in smelling wonderful as he always did of Ettienne Aigner aftershave. He had a very commanding physical presence, tall with broad shoulders and very dark hair. His eyes were a hazily brown colour and you could read his mood just by looking into them. His clothes were always immaculate whatever the occasion. He had told her he derived his dark looks from his father as he was Italian, and his mother was Scottish.

She'd met Samuel at university many years ago and they had stayed friends, sharing the same humour and interests in art and music. Samuel had a wonderful voice and sang in the university choir while Veronica loved being part of the drama society. When they left university, they had stayed in touch, always there for each other, when he went through a painful divorce and when Veronica needed a shoulder to cry on over one of her disastrous boyfriends. They had shared so much, they became almost like brother and sister and could tell each other just about anything which didn't leave any opening for each other as partners. She knew he had been seeing someone recently but surprisingly he had kept this relationship under wraps. She thought he'd tell her when he was ready. She hadn't seen anyone in over two years after a disastrous and quite angry break up from Peter, so she wasn't really looking for a relationship, she was quite happy on her own as she kept telling herself.

Samuel threw himself down on her couch after giving her his customary bear hug and asked her if she would like to accompany him to a music concert the following evening. What's wrong with taking the flavour of the moment she teased him, he raised his eyebrow and his dark eyes twinkled.

Amused, he said "I don't know what you mean, you know I only have eyes for you". He asked her if her lecture had gone well at university and she told him how thankful she was that he had persuaded her to do it. They chatted some more and then arranged to meet up at the theatre entrance at 8pm the following evening. When he had left, Veronica thought about what to wear, she enjoyed her evenings out with Samuel, it gave her chance to dress up a bit and she went and had a look through her evening wear.

Georgina shouted "Hi" as she came through the house door expecting her husband to be home as it was an early finish day at work and his turn to cook dinner in which he excelled. She couldn't smell any cooking going on and realised he wasn't home. Disappointed and with a doubtful feeling niggling in her stomach, she took off her shoes and coat and started looking at what she could muscle up for dinner. This had been happening quite often recently. Her dependable husband was becoming less so and little things didn't add up; he wasn't always where she expected him to be. Not that she kept tabs on him, but she called his mobile and it went on to the answerphone, "Maybe he had to stay late at work," she thought.

They had been very young when married and had a teenage daughter, Grace, who was studying Photography at university. She was coming home at the weekend and had said she would be bringing a friend with her which she was rather secretive about, but they had always encouraged her to bring her friends home, being an only child. Nothing to be done, she would make dinner and leave Robin's in the oven and hope he turned up before it dried out. Two hours later, she heard the door open and Robin put his head around the door saying "Sorry love, got a bit tied up with work, just going upstairs to shower, shan't be a tick" and with that he bounded upstairs leaving her with a confused look on her face.

Georgina had fallen for Robin's cheerful nature when she first met him as a teenager. He was very sporty and had played tennis and cycled for as long as she knew him. His tall frame with fair hair and easy manner made it easy for her to fall in love with him and he was the only boyfriend she'd ever had. When she thought how their lives had changed and their relationship with each other, it saddened her. Robin had gone to work in an accounting firm which at the time seemed a good, safe job but in hindsight, she knew it didn't suit his nature and he should have stuck out for something that involved sports or activities coaching. She had decided to go into teaching and then found out she was pregnant, so they had married and she thought things would be fine. They had been until recently.

Over dinner, she reminded him that Grace was bringing a friend home for the weekend and Robin said that he'd forgotten and had arranged to meet up for a game of tennis at the club with Michael who he doubled up with. Feeling let down again, she got up from the table and left the dishes for him to clear and went to bed. She laid in bed trying to unclutter her confused brain and put a finger on what was niggling her, just some strange gut feeling, she resolved she would sit down with him and try to sort out what it was.

Robin started filling the dishwasher wondering what he was going to do about his life. Things were getting more complicated and Georgina was becoming suspicious. He would have to leave early in the morning, or she would try to pin him down with questions he wasn't ready to answer. He scratched his head and ran his hand through his hair, and thought, yes, that would take care of the morning, I'll work something out tomorrow. He smiled to himself and glanced at his reflection in the mirror, thinking he'd call in for a haircut tomorrow and treat himself to a massage, things weren't so bad. He'd had a bit of a fright when he had spotted Veronica in Times restaurant at lunch but luckily managed to nip out and get a table around the corner at Bistro O'Neal's and rearrange his lunch date in time. He wasn't very hungry at dinner after such a lovely lunch, but he thought he'd have a quick watch of TV then go to bed and Georgina would be asleep by then.

Georgina rose early in the morning, but not early enough to talk to Robin who'd gone out very early and left her a note to say he was going to do some catching up at work and he'd see her later.

CHAPTER THREE

Georgina drove her treasured, red sports car to school and as she did, she thought about the day ahead, she was an English Teacher and she loved her job. She hoped to see her friend Judith at lunch time to have a chat with her and maybe arrange a night out at the theatre or something.

Georgina sat with Judith in the staff canteen and while munching on their lunch, she told her what she was worrying about. They were very different in personality, Georgina being very active and articulate with her reading and routine life and was tall and fair whereas Judith was small with mousy hair and very relaxed about her work routine which helped Georgina to chill in her company. They were discussing what was the best course of action to help Billy who they both taught to become more involved in their lessons and decided to arrange a field day out with half a dozen of children from the class and take them to Castleton in Derbyshire to visit one of the caves, then get them to write a story about it afterwards.

They arranged the trip because nothing else they had tried with Billy had made any difference to his behaviour in the classroom. The following Saturday, they'd managed to get permission for five of the children to go on the trip including Billy. The day went very well apart from losing Billy for a spell when he decided he'd missed a bit of the cave and wandered back on the track. They soon found him though and they were all sitting, enjoying the sunshine with a picnic at the top of Winnit's Pass. The children were asking lots of questions about the cave which the guide had taken them around. He had really stirred up their imagination with stories of the tunnel collapsing and ghosts. Billy said "I saw a ghost when I went down a tunnel on my own" then he started running after the other children with his hands in the air pretending to be one which got them all very excited and wore them out chasing around.

Georgina's daughter, Grace, shared a flat with Judith's daughter, Imogen so they often chatted about their daughters and the courses they were on at university. Judith had two other children who resembled her although Imogen must take after her husband, Georgina thought as she was tall and dark and very attractive. They finished their day with ice creams then made their way home, dropping off the children. They had chatted all the way home and Billy had been in fine form, seeming to have made a friend of little Jinny who was quite a handful herself when she felt like it but kept Billy in his place. Funny how things work out Georgina thought. The children were told to prepare their stories for next week and a prize would be given for the best story.

CHAPTER FOUR

As soon as Billy arrived home from Castleton, he threw his coat off and bounded up the stairs to his bedroom. His mother shouted up at him asking if he'd had a nice time and when she got no answer, she went up to his room and couldn't believe her eyes. Billy was emptying bits of stones and rocks out of his pockets and placing them on his windowsill. He told her he'd picked them up on the cave floor and they were probably very old fossils, possibly bits of stalactites. Billy's mother smiled doubting very much their authenticity but delighted to see Billy so animated. She worked full time as a cleaner and had very little spare money for treats for Billy, having three children and being a single parent. She had no help from Billy's dad. It had affected Billy much more than his two younger siblings when his father left as the other two were too young to understand and Billy missed his father. He had grown very sullen and difficult as he got older, resenting the other children at school who seemed to have so much more. She had been called into school on more than one occasion, the cause being his bad behaviour which had been slowly getting worse. To see him grabbing paper and a pen, sitting at his table scribbling away it nearly took her breath away with relief. He told her he was going to write about his day in Castleton and there was a prize for the best story. He said big Charlie Thompson said he was going to win the competition, but Jinny said she thought he was rubbish and she had more chance than him. She smiled and wondered who Jinny was as he went on to chat happily about his day mentioning her name several times.

She closed the door behind her after telling him dinner would be ready in an hour, but she doubted he heard her because he already had his head down scratching away on his story. She felt very thankful to Billy's teachers who had taken him out for the day trip, she called him later to come down and get his tea, but it took her another hour before he came down. He said he was going to call in the library on the way home from school the next day to find some more information out. She was astounded, it was like suddenly having another child in the family. His siblings tormented him and said they thought he had a crush on Jinny when she arrived back home with him the following day to research and write their stories together.

Judith and Georgina had read the stories that the children had written. They had both decided who the winner would be not only because of the content but also because of the way it was composed. When Judith stood in front of the class and declared the winner of the best story, she said they all had been very good and she'd enjoyed reading them, but the one they had chosen was Billy's because of its different slant on the caves they all visited and made them feel as though they were actually there.

Billy's chest rose with such pride and he really felt like crying. He had hoped he would win but didn't expect to do as he had never won anything in his life and good things like that happened to other people not him. He had studied and read about the lives of people who had worked in the caves in Castleton; how so many had died when the caves collapsed or flooded; and when he had disappeared for a short time on his own during the visit, how he had felt quite spooky and disconnected and was glad to return to the group. He made his story about the men and their work and enjoyed describing their hard surroundings and everyday fears that they had to work through. The prize he won was a family ticket to the caves which could be used at any time. Billy couldn't wait until the end of the school day to get home and tell his mum he had won. He ran in the door and burst out with what had happened and his mother was so delighted she could have cried. She looked at her son's happy, smiling face and felt very thankful, Billy had such a wonderful teacher who had managed to unlock her son's imagination. She would write a letter of thanks to the school and told Billy that Jinny could come as well when they went to the caves with their winning tickets which made his smile even bigger.

Judith and Georgina really saw a change in Billy, he still had his moments but was quite taken with all things geological and they found more books for him to read with this in mind. They both decided to make more trips of the same kind in the future.

CHAPTER FIVE

Grace ran along the shopping mall, once outside, she ran along the tree lined road which she loved with all the huge branches above blowing in the breeze, until she reached her apartment steps taking them two at a time. Her long, blonde hair cascaded around her excited face. She had just bought a new outfit and wanted to try it all on before her room mates, Imogen and Bertie arrived back. Grace was studying photography with Business studies while Bertie was on a Drama course and Imogen was taking Art and Design. She thought how different they all were and how lucky they were to be sharing their flat together. Grace was organised and made sure all the bills were paid, Imogen was very creative and enjoyed making dinners and cakes but was a bit messy and Bertie loved to tidy up and clean but could get a little hyped up sometimes as he was very sensitive. He was learning a script and would practice his lines in front of the girls for their thoughts on his performance which they were very careful not to say the wrong thing.

Grace stood in front of the mirror and thought she had done well, the green felt hat and large slouchy belt with her leggings and tunic looked great and a bit between Maid Marion and Robin Hood. She would wear this at the weekend when she went home. She had invited Carl, Bertie's Drama coach on the pretext of going to a performance of 'The Black Widow' which was showing at the theatre near her parents. She'd been on a few dates with Carl, but mainly with other people. He was handsome in a quirky way and very unpredictable, not what you would expect from a university lecturer. He was laid back with curly, dark hair, tall and slim and quite an inventive dresser. Anyway, she thought she'd see how the weekend went, not knowing whether things would go one way or another. He was extremely complimentary, but things were going very slowly.

Imogen pushed the front door open and shoved her bags along the hall floor while she closed it. Her long dark hair was pulled back in a scrunchie. Imogen was tall and attractive with long dark auburn hair and olive skin, a bit like a young Sophie Lauren. She shouted 'Hi" and carried the bags of shopping into the kitchen and started to empty them out into the cupboards as Bertie came into the kitchen and started to help her. Bertie was quite stocky and fair haired with an angelic face and open smile. He smiled when he saw the cherries and almonds, realising that Imogen was going to be making his favourite cherry and almond scones which usually came with jam and clotted cream.

Bertie had been delighted when he'd seen the advertisement for the flat share and found he would be sharing with the two girls, they had all got on so well with from the start, all having the same sort of courses in the Arts. Bertie hadn't had it too easy when he was a young boy at school, being on the brunt of much bullying which often started when the children learned his surname. The teacher would read out his name in the morning attendance register "Bertram Alcock" and Bertie would whisper "Here". There was often a murmur of tittering to be heard until the teacher shouted "Silence!" When he came home from school, often bruised and cut from fighting in the playground, his mother used to worry so much, until one day he came home with a big smile on his face to tell his mother he was going to be in the school play and they had given him a main part in 'Guys and Dolls'. From then on, Bertie knew what he wanted to do and applied to Drama school where everyone there were characters and as unique as he was. Now when he went for auditions and they asked his name, he put emphasis on the 'All' at the beginning of his surname which usually raised an eyebrow from the producers and a smile from the directors. But it had stood him in good stead.

When Grace came through from the living room and they both exclaimed "Crikey O Riley, what are you wearing, you look great, what's the occasion?" She smiled and said "I'm just trying my outfit on

for the weekend. Do you think he'll like it?"
"What's not to like honey" trilled Bertie, "Quite
sexy in a Sherwood Forest kind of way!" Bertie had
introduced Grace to Carl in the pub after a concert,
he didn't know much about him apart from his
tutoring at university but was surprised when he'd
hit it off with Grace, as she had been on her own
a while after a disastrous affair with a guy who
both Imogen and he disliked and was glad when it
ended. He just hoped she'd take it slowly and not
fall madly in love with him until she found out
more about him.

Bertie had been so surprised when Carl had
started taking an interest in Grace, not that she
wasn't a very attractive girl, but he thought that he
would have had more chance with him, "Funny
how you could get it so wrong" he thought. Bertie
didn't have a partner and hadn't really had anyone
special in his life. He'd had a bit of a crush on a boy
in high school but that was about it. He loved his
music and theatre; Judy Garland, Abba, and his
mum, that was enough for him and he was a happy
chap, not looking for love in any other way.

Imogen was the eldest of three children, her
two siblings were nothing like her, favouring her
mother's fair skin. She often wondered how she
could look so different. She loved her art course
and hoped to make a living from it when she left
university, but she was trying to find her core self
to express her artwork and create a different

prospective to her work so her work would be recognised by its uniqueness. She tried many forms of adding paint to her canvas to bring her work to life and loved the journey of creating an atmospheric piece of art which would reflect the scenery around her. She went for long walks with her sketch pad and paints slung over her shoulder and would find beauty in all sorts of landscape. She loved the autumn and the colours of reds and golds as summer began to sleep and autumn blanketed the ground when walking through the woods at Langsett and around the reservoir, breathing in the rich, leafy smells and feeling grateful to have such beautiful surroundings. She loved her art course and had set an easel up in the room where she had a full table laid out for her art projects. She was curiously experimenting with oils on canvas, deep bright orange and purples making waterfalls fall out of stars and loving it. It was a very special piece and only her two flat mates had seen it. The canvas was 5 foot by 5 foot and almost filled one wall. She had been working on it for weeks, but she just needed something else to add to it, but not sure what it was. She was hoping to exhibit it at the gallery at Fourth Street as they were having an open week for new artists in three weeks' time. The winner would be entered into a main gallery in London.

Grace packed her small bag for the weekend and sat and waited for Carl to arrive and take her to her parents, she was excited and kept checking her hair and makeup, not too much, preferring a natural look. She played with her camera which was like an extension of her arm and always with her. The doorbell went and Bertie opened the door and Grace took a picture of Carl in the door frame, the light from the wall light fitment twinkled in his curly, dark hair, she smiled as he hugged her and said, "You ready?" and off they went to his open topped MR2 and sped away.

They chatted away on the journey to her parents, Grace had been surprised when Carl had asked her out initially. He was quite a bit older than her, but she felt flattered and went along because she wasn't seeing anyone else and he did compliment her and make her feel good, although she did find him very secretive. He asked her lots of questions about her parents and where she lived and was quite surprised when he accepted her invitation to her home and to the theatre.

CHAPTER SIX

Veronica saw Samuel at the top of the theatre steps before he saw her. She admired his tall, dark looks which he took from his father's side of the family as his father was Italian and his mother Scottish. He had a long camel coat over his suit and was immaculately dressed. She'd opted for a calf length skirt and red silk blouse that she knew suited her colouring with a small brooch; with her hair curled gently to her shoulders which made her look very attractive. He kissed her cheek and said, "You look good enough to eat" and led her to their seats. He'd bought the programme and she excitedly waited for the lights to dim and the music to begin. She looked sideways at his profile and felt a stirring of pleasure looking at his handsome face and thought how lucky she was to have him in her life. How different this might have been if she'd told him what had happened to her all those years ago when she was just seventeen. Anyway, 'water under the bridge' now, there's only now and now was good. She pushed the dark thought away and gave herself up to the music.

After the concert, he drove her home and she asked if he wanted a night cap. He said "Ok, just a quickie" with a twinkle in his eye and as she poured his whiskey, he pressed the music on and pulled her into his arms while Frank Sinatra purred away to "Some enchanted evening." As they sashayed around her apartment, laughing, she pulled away from him and said, "I think it must be home time for you oh handsome one", he looked at her with a dark, unfathomable look in his eyes, then smiled and said, "I think it is!"

Samuel walked slowly down the steps to his car thinking about Veronica. Strange, he thought as close as they were, there was always an invisible barrier between them which stopped them taking a step beyond their friendship. He thought back to his first meeting of Veronica all those years ago at the party and how he had woken up the next morning to find her gone. They had never spoken of it and he felt she regretted it. They had both drunk far too much and one thing had led to another. Maybe, he thought it was more because they had known each other for so long. He jumped into his car and turned the music on full and thought of the song they'd just danced around her flat to, "Some enchanted evening' had always been their song. He sped home to his bachelor pad which was at the other side of town and not so much a pad, as a very elegant house. He'd lived there some time and had bought it after his divorce and changed it to his liking, spending much on renovations and landscaping the surrounding gardens. Veronica tormented him, saying he thought he was 'Lord of the Manor' rattling around in his large house. Samuel enjoyed the fruits of his hard labour. He had to work very hard after his divorce settlement and without his wife anymore, who liked to spend freely of his money, he was doing very well for himself. He concentrated on his business portfolio and was kept more than busy keeping a firm hand on the till.

Meanwhile, Veronica lay alone, also thinking back to when she was seventeen years old and finding herself pregnant after the university party she had gone to with all her friends. She'd thought back to the shock of waking up in the strange, dark room not knowing where she was to begin with, or even who's arm was laid over her. She remembered looking back at the bedroom door and seeing Samuel's face and for some reason, she didn't know why, but it made her feel better. She'd made her way back to her flat not really thinking much about it until three months later, realising she was pregnant and it could only have been Samuel's baby as she had a stern talk to herself afterwards. Also, now Samuel was seeing someone else and she didn't want him to know. It was just a stupid mistake and she'd have to sort it out.

The only thing she could think to do at the time was to go home to her Aunt Rosie's and decide what to do then. She knew she couldn't really keep the baby, but she couldn't bear to think about it just yet. Her Aunt Rosie had brought her up from a baby and when her parents who were both Botanists, travelled abroad which was most of the time. Rosie looked after her and when they moved to a position in Africa, Rosie became her full-time trustee. Her parents paid for her boarding school education and when both Alice and Oliver, Rosie's sister and brother-in-law were on a small plane, travelling to a remote part of Africa, their plane had come down and there were no survivors. Veronica had been only very young when Rosie gently told her that her parents had died in a plane crash. Veronica took the news well as she had had very little contact with them, Rosie had always been her mother figure, so when Veronica had turned up at Rosie's looking lost and frightened, Rosie had put her arms around her and said, 'Don't worry, we'll sort this out together.'

CHAPTER SEVEN

Rosie was much younger than her sister, Alice. She looked up to her sister, thinking her so clever and worldly and when she married Oliver, who was very charming and also worked as a Botanist, she saw little of her eldest sister as they travelled with their research abroad a lot.

Their parents were very conventional. Her father, Thomas, was the village Postman and her mother looked after the children. Alice started showing signs from an early age of being very bright and it was no surprise to anyone that she went to university which was quite rare at that time, especially for girls. She met Oliver on a field trip in Italy and married very young. They both went into the same line of work studying plant life which took them far afield. Rosy had come along quite a while after her sister and she looked up to her, so when she worked away for long spells, she missed her. Alice had been working with Oliver in South Africa for 6 months when it was arranged for Rosie to go and visit her. Rosie was beside herself with excitement, only just 17 years old and never been abroad before, it was a long flight and her parents had been anxious about her flying alone, but Alice had said she would meet her in Cape Town and that Rosie wouldn't be left alone.

Rosie loved her first week there but by the second week she couldn't wait to get home. She arrived back home a different girl to when she went and her parents thought it was probably her age but as the weeks passed by, she became much more miserable, Alice was arriving back in England for a new project with Oliver and it was decided that she would go to stay with them for a while and Rosie got a job in the local art gallery.

Rosie was very 'arty', always a free spirit, she had dropped out of college upon returning from her trip abroad, but she did enjoy her job in the art gallery. Alice having a baby was one of the reasons Alice and Oliver returned to England. Rosie helped Alice look after the baby and when she resumed her work, Rosie took on the role of nanny permanently. When Alice and Oliver went back to South Africa, baby Veronica was left with Rosie and they paid her to care for the baby. Rosie loved looking after Veronica and it was decided she would go to boarding school when she was older and she would see her in the school holidays.

During this time, Rosie had a relationship with a fellow artist who lived with her for a while and they had a child together called Georgina, so Veronica and Georgina grew up together, although Veronica went into boarding school and Georgina went to mainstream school. Georgina excelled academically and went on to get a Degree and become a teacher. Rosie's partner didn't stay long after baby Georgina arrived and went off to find himself working on different projects. Rosie lost contact with him which didn't bother her because the relationship had run its course, but she was grateful she had Georgina from their time together and the two children grew up together.

Although so different in personalities, Veronica was creative and artistic and Georgina being practical and logical and very bright at school. She wondered how Veronica would fare in the world as she didn't really fit in too well at her boarding school, flitting and floating from one class to another. Veronica was artistic and loved poetry whereas Georgina was a tomboy and loved to climb trees and would stand her ground in an argument and not be trodden on.

When Alice and Oliver died in the accident, Rosie carried on as before. She had now returned to painting and had established her artwork in various galleries and made a decent living. When Veronica turned up from university unannounced one weekend with a worried look on her face, it didn't take Rosie long to guess her predicament. She really didn't know how she was going to be able to help look after another baby as she was so much older, so when Veronica said she wanted to have the baby adopted, she went along with it as the best option and helped her. Veronica didn't want anyone to know about her pregnancy and luckily Georgina was away studying in France on a school programme at the time so when she returned, Veronica was back at university and Georgina was none the wiser. Rosie had felt bad keeping the secret from her but went along with Veronica's wishes as she just wanted to put it all behind her and thought the less people who knew, the better.

Rosie was with Veronica when she gave birth to her baby daughter and as she looked into the tiny baby's dark eyes and dark hair, she felt a deep sense of love and sadness. She took a picture of them as they slept and when the baby was taken to her new parents, she vowed to find out where she had gone. Rosy had been in turmoil when Veronica had insisted on letting her baby daughter go for adoption, but she had no choice but to go along with her wishes after Veronica went back to university to finish her degree. Rosie found out where the baby had gone and visited the village where she was living. She called in the small café in the village of Tideswell and was soon chatting to the local ladies who frequented the café and found out all she needed to know about a couple who lived in a large house at the top of the village. Their new baby had a nanny to look after their child called Judith. They told her that Judith called in the café on a Thursday on the way back from the library with baby Imogen. After that, Rosie made regular visits to the coffee shop on Thursdays and struck up conversations with Judith, only to find after several months that Judith stopped coming and the locals in the coffee shop told Rosie she had moved back to her hometown in Buxton. Rosie enquired further and found out the wife of the couple who had adopted Imogen had died and no one seemed to know where baby Imogen had gone. They suspected that Judith had her and she was probably the biological mother from a liaison with the husband.

Rosie decided to travel to Buxton to see if she could find where Judith had gone with Imogen. She couldn't just leave things the way they were, never knowing what had happened to her so she went over to Buxton and found a very nice Bed and Breakfast in the centre of the Old Spa town and decided to make it a little holiday. She had a good look around and got to know the place better. There were splendid shops in a small arcade which sold quite unusual merchandise and a wonderful art gallery as well as a very old theatre which she could see was very popular with tourists as well as locals.

The first morning, Rosie rose and had a delicious breakfast which the landlady called Marian had cooked for her and when she finished, she asked her where the famous spa water could be found and Marian told her it was at the side of the park.

Rosie asked her for directions and thought that would be a good place to start her search as she knew most mothers liked to walk in the park with their prams. When Rosie arrived at the park gates, she noticed there was a library at the side and thought she'd pop in there after her walk. There were many young girls and couples with children and prams enjoying the lovely day in the park and Rosie was beginning to think she was on a wild goose chase when she looked over by the duck pond and saw to her delight, Judith in the distance with a man by her side pushing the pram. He was a nice-looking man and was laughing with her and she could see baby Imogen sat up beaming at them. Rosie kept well back from the little trio because she didn't want her presence to be known but thought how lucky she was to have found them. When later in the day Rosie returned to her bed and breakfast, she asked Marian if she knew of Judith, thinking it was a long shot but also knew how local people got to know one another. Marian was well known in the area having lived there from being a child and said it was her friend's daughter who'd recently come home with a baby and was seeing someone called Stephen, a local man who ran the estate agent in town.

Rosie saw Judith a couple more times still from a distance during her stay and when she returned home, she kept in touch with Marian whom she had become friends with and was happy when she heard that Judith was getting married and expecting another child. It saddened Rosie all the same. She went home and carried on with her life and Veronica never mentioned her baby again.

CHAPTER EIGHT

Georgina and Veronica were devastated when they received a call from the police to say that Rosie's next-door neighbour had found Rosie's body. The neighbour had thought she was asleep in her chair, but she had passed away. Rosie had always been a larger-than-life character and led such a full life, so it was a shock to them both. She had no health worries that they knew of and it seemed that she had simply fallen asleep and not woken up.

The ride over to the Rosie's cottage led Veronica and Georgina up a long winding lane where they parked their car on the grass verge in front of the cottage. It was a very pretty, white painted house which at one time had been an old schoolhouse. The bell up on the roof still hung there which would have been rung many years ago to call in the children to class. It had a very pretty garden surrounding it which Rosie spent many happy hours tending to. The front of the house was covered in a wonderful lilac Wisteria which framed the windows. As they opened the door and stepped inside, they couldn't believe that Rosie wouldn't be there fussing around them and plying them with tea and cakes and wanting to know all their gossip. Everything was just as before, her easel stood with an unfinished painting on it and her book laid open by her chair with her glasses.

Later, when they were sorting Rosie's belongings out, they carefully packed her bright coloured scarfs and clothes for the charity shop. They reminisced over how she had her long, red hair up in bits of colourful material and how amazing she used to look in the clothes she often created in brightly coloured fabrics. Veronica held a long green and orange velvet skirt up and said, "I'm going to keep this, I can't bear to let it go, even if I never wear it, I might have the material made into cushion covers." It was Rosie's favourite skirt and she wore it often when she was painting. Georgina kept a small scarf pin which she pinned to her blouse and they both kept a ring each. Veronica's ring had a stone of Whitby Jet and Georgina's had a blue Sapphire.

They decided to have a pub lunch after the nostalgic morning. Georgina had taken a box of old photographs to go through at home and put them in her car. She was always very busy, working full time teaching and her daughter, Grace had just started university and she had been helping her find accommodation. Also, her husband Robin kept her on her toes, always moaning how he hated his job as an accountant. Luckily Veronica didn't live very far away so they met up quite often. Veronica had studied at Sheffield University and had a flat nearby whereas Georgina had stayed near to Oughtibridge in Sheffield.

As they both talked about Rosie's life and how she had helped them both in so many ways, neither of them could understand why she had gone so early on in her life. They talked of how magical she made their country walks when they were young and the special picnics she made from the most unusual ingredients; the bilberry and blackberry picking; and, looking for fairies in the woods. They used to collect acorns from an old oak tree and Rosy used to say the cup of the acorn was a fairy cup. They both had magical memories of her.

CHAPTER NINE

Veronica was on the way to Glen Howe Park which was one of the places Rosie had taken her and Georgina as children and they had spent many hours playing there in the woods. In the centre of the park was an old house with a castellated roof where a school friend of Georgina's used to live as her parents were caretakers of the park. They were called Vera and Cecil and she recalled Vera used to make teas and cakes in a café which adjoined the house while Cecil worked in the grounds. There was a tennis court at the top end of the glen and they used to hire out tennis rackets to groups of people and book the court out. The park had a stream running through which had trout in and there was a lovely old stone bridge which crossed the river called The Packhorse Bridge. She and Georgina had spent hours on the bridge spotting fish and playing stick where they threw a stick over one side of the bridge and ran to the other side to see it bobbing down the river. She smiled with the wonderful memories of picnics in the sweet smelling, blue bell woods and how Rosie used to say the fairies made some of the blue bells ring and how long they spent looking for one that rang and never gave up hope.

Vera got used to seeing them both paddling in the river with their dog Bessy. She once showed them a secret room in the house which was behind a patterned papered wall that moved away and revealed a hidden stairway up the tower to a small room within the tower. She used it as a small bedroom for her daughter Rosalie. Georgina had thought this was amazing as she was really into the 'Famous Five' books which fuelled her imagination. Veronica remembered hearing Cecil whistling away while he worked, clearing the woods and crafting wonderful wooden huts from the branches. They had benches inside them where you could shelter when it rained and also to keep away from midges when eating picnics. She thought then of Rosie's picnics with all the little surprises wrapped in parcels. They were very happy times. The park used to be awash with colour in the spring from the Rhododendron and Azaleas and carpets of Snowdrops and Bluebells.

It had been many years since she had visited the park but with Rosie's passing, she suddenly wanted a trip down memory lane. She thought it had probably changed as Vera and Cecil were long gone. She had parked in the car park at the bottom of the lane to the entrance and noticed there were no other cars or people around as she walked through the open gate. She looked ahead and saw a large hare sat in the middle of the lane on its hind legs. They both looked at each other then the hare hopped ahead along the path and disappeared into the woods. She carried on up the lane to the house, sadly noting the obvious neglect to the wooded gardens. The Rhododendron were covered with branches from broken trees and it was obvious there was very little, if any, maintenance being carried out on the grounds. She wondered what had happened. She knew it had been many years since she visited and much could happen in a short time if nature was left to its own devices. On reaching the house in the woods, she was amazed and dismayed to see just how bad things had become. There was a tree branch growing from the roof of the house that Vera was once so proud of and the windows were all but hanging in there. Trees overshadowed the whole building, making the once fairy castle into more of a dungeon.

Everything had taken over and been left unattended and the result was very depressing. An elderly man was walking down from the top bridge with his dog and said, "Good morning" He told Veronica that the council had taken over the running of the park and didn't have the money to preserve it, leaving the house unloved and distressed. She spoke for a while with the gentleman reminiscing the past and then he went on his way.

As she walked up to the place where the tennis courts used to be, she thought she saw a figure of a young girl in front of her but when she looked again, she saw nothing but the large hare leaping over a broken tree bough. She found what she had half expected – that the tennis court was long gone and just as overgrown as the rest of the grounds. She walked back down to the house where the tearoom was no longer in evidence either. Thoughtfully, she returned to her car with a germ of an idea twinkling in her head, while the hare stood on his hind legs and watched her drive away.

CHAPTER TEN

Grace thought the weekend had gone quite well to begin with and the play was very good. She had hardly seen her father as he was out playing tennis and her mother made a lovely dinner on their arrival. All was going very well until her father arrived later and she introduced him to Carl. Her father acted very strange and was, Grace thought, very abrupt with him before going out again, saying he had to go into work to sort things out. That was all she saw of him and Carl seemed to be out of sorts after that and just pecked her cheek when he dropped her off at the flat then sped off. She went in and Imogen plied her with questions and sensed things weren't quite right but didn't push her. Bertie was unusually quiet too.

Grace busied herself with her course work. She was working on interlocking art with her photography and she took some pictures of Imogen as they walked together through the tree lined road with the leaves turning to rich autumn colours of red and gold. Imogen's beautiful, long, dark auburn hair with the reds and gold around her and the path like a red and gold river, she couldn't wait to get back and look at the pictures and see what she could do with them.

Imogen had started seeing a guy she had met in a gallery and they had been to a couple of art exhibitions and lectures together. She found him very good company and liked that he was experienced in a 'worldly' way without being 'showy'. He was thoughtful and caring but she didn't look on him as anything other than an older man who she enjoyed the company of now and then.

Imogen's mother, Judith, was on her way to meet Georgina for a lunch date and she wondered if she had sorted her worry out about her husband. She herself had had her share of worries in her past and thought back to when she was young and worked for a couple as their baby's nanny and how attached she had become to the baby. She remembered how devastated the husband had been when his wife died suddenly and left him with the child, a small baby with no mother. He had begged Judith to look after the child as her own as he just didn't want the adopted child anymore without his wife.

Judith had gone home and passed the child off as her own to her parents, implying that it was the result of an affair she had had with her employee. After marrying Stephen, who was very good with baby Imogen and treated her as his own, they had gone on to have two more children. She never told Imogen and worried about it, but she had left it so long that she thought it better to 'let sleeping dogs lie'. She had gone on to college as a mature student when the children were older and now worked as a teacher at her local school. She loved her job and it had fitted in well with the children and their school holidays.

Georgina was waiting for her with a worried look on her face, but she smiled when she saw her. As they waited for their food order, she told Judith about Robin's strange behaviour and how he had reacted to Grace's boyfriend, Carl. She said it had been quite embarrassing because Robin was so rude and left as soon as he'd arrived, saying that he had to go back to work for some emergency, but she was pretty sure he had made it up. She felt that it was awkward for Grace and that he acted so selfishly, she just didn't know what to think, confessing that he had started preening himself in front of the mirror and buying new clothes which he'd never done before, Georgina wondered if he was having a fling with the new secretary in his office, but he was always saying that she was a pain in the neck and clock-watching him.

Judith listened to her friend rambling on and said "Well, fathers can act quite jealously when their daughters start getting boyfriends and bringing them home, maybe it's making him feel old." but privately, she did think it sounded fishy too. Georgina said she doubted he was jealous, then their food was served and they had another glass of wine. Georgina relaxed a little and when she left, she felt a little happier. They said their goodbyes and that they would see each other at work on Monday.

CHAPTER ELEVEN

Imogen was working on her painting and adding light to the background to bring the stars out more in the painting when Grace burst in with her arms full of pictures to show her friend which she had taken of Imogen. One picture stood out of Imogen which was taken as the wind blew her hair like a halo around her head mixing in with the autumn leaves which made her hair look copper and gold and quite ethereal. She looked at her friend as she stood in front of her huge painting of stars and waterfalls and a thought took place which excited her, but she decided to keep it to herself for the time being.

When Imogen had gone out the next morning, Grace photographed her friend's painting then worked all afternoon with her proofs until she had the results she'd been looking for. She could hardly believe the feeling she had as she looked at it, thinking about her friend's reaction. She had combined Imogen's oil painting and her own picture which had created a unique amalgam of the two contrasting artists. She wondered what Imogen would think and hoped she approved.

Imogen was at her art class when a visiting artist came over to her table and looked over her shoulder to view her work. She had been experimenting with her blues and reds and couldn't quite get the look she wanted. She was looking for the extra ingredient to put into her secret picture at home which she wanted to add to the exhibition competition at the gallery. The artist was a woman who was a mature student that Imogen hadn't noticed before, so she presumed that she was a visitor. She looked to be in her mid-thirties and dressed quite 'arty' with a long skirt in a vintage pattern. As she walked by, she accidentally caught Imogen's chair which spilt grey paint across her canvas and with dismay, Imogen watched as the grey paint trickled across the crevices of her painting, but then she gasped with awe at the look that it gave, which was a pattern of ethereal light and shade. She turned to the woman, but she must have gone from the room and she didn't see her again for the rest of the class.

Imogen couldn't wait to go home and use this new mix on her own picture and when she arrived back, she burst into her art room in the flat and threw her bags down and started mixing her paints. She mixed the grey with a little silver and white - the same mix as on her course work and started to add the paint to her huge canvas. She started in the top left corner and carefully touched the old, dried paintwork with her new formula and stood back. She smiled to herself and felt a tingling sense of joy.

She then applied the same to each corner, bringing the paint towards the centre in each corner of her canvas. The new paint added a different essence of colour and light. The top left made her stars and waterfalls of her original painting seem light and bright and added a hint of fresh new lime green. The top right was much brighter, still almost a hint of yellow sparkling from her stars and sliding down the waterfalls. The bottom left was a rich with reds and golds and purples and the bottom right was silvery grey with just a twinkle of red, all coming together in the centre like a huge volcano of stars. She stood back from her painting after working on it for two days and she saw the title of her painting immediately, 'Four Seasons', because that's what she had created – Spring, Summer, Autumn and Winter in all four corners of her work, manifesting into a whole year in the centre.

Meanwhile, Grace was also wondering if her friend would allow her to enter her photograph printed on her friend's canvas into the competition, or if she should just enter the one of Imogen walking through the leaves individually. There was no doubt in her mind that the combination of the dark autumn artwork of Imogen's and Imogen seemingly walking among the stars was the better of the two. She would have to see how things went.

Grace went into the flat and Imogen asked her to look at her finished picture. She told Grace about the woman who'd been in class and spilt paint on her canvas which gave her the idea. Grace looked at her friend's picture with shock as she saw the huge difference and changes she had made which made the canvas seem like a living thing, quite amazing and nothing like the original she had photographed. Grace kept her photograph to herself for the time being, the competition was in two weeks and the work had to be entered by then so she had time to think what she should do.

Grace hadn't seen anything of Carl since the weekend away and guessed things were off with him. She got on with her work but wondered why. She had heard he was seeing someone else through her flat mate Bertie, but he wasn't giving much away, he was busy playing his part in 'The Inspector Calls' and enjoying himself. He had secretly found Carl attractive, but thought he wasn't in is field, although from what he had heard recently, he had been wrong about that. He thought it wouldn't do for Grace to find out, so he thought he'd keep it to himself. Carl had been to watch Bertie in his play and taken him for dinner afterwards which gave Bertie hope, but Carl was very secretive, and Bertie felt sure he had something or someone 'up his sleeve'.

Meanwhile, Robin was walking a fine line. He'd always known he was attracted to men as well as women, but he had married Georgina, thinking he would forget all that side of things and concentrate on his career and hopefully grow out of it. Then he met Carl at the tennis club and he had completely fallen for him. He'd been meeting up with Carl for months and wasn't really looking ahead but just going along with it. Things with Georgina had grown stale over the last few years and Robin thought that they were never much more than good friends and that things should have stopped there but things just seemed to happen and before he knew it, he was married with a baby.

He had been shaken to the core when Grace had brought Carl home for the weekend. He couldn't believe his eyes and had to get out of the room as soon as he could. Carl had said afterwards that he had no idea that Grace was his daughter, but it had made Robin cool things off and want to sort his life out. He knew that Carl wasn't looking for a permanent relationship and that he was a bit of a free spirit, but he wasn't going to 'rain on his parade' with Grace. He had heard it was over between Carl and Grace, so he was very relieved.

CHAPTER TWELVE

Samuel was waiting for Veronica at their usual Thursday lunchtime restaurant when he spotted an attractive older woman staring over at him from the corner of the restaurant. She was wearing a beautiful antique shawl over her shoulder and had her hair loosely bound up. Veronica arrived then breathless, a little late and kissed his cheek. He thought how lovely she always looked and how effortlessly she threw her clothes together which made a statement in a classical, yet 'arty' way. She settled down to look at the menu and he forgot the other woman. Veronica told Samuel all about her visit to the glen and how badly everything had been neglected. She added that she had some ideas and was going to put them to the local council to see if there was some way of using the park area to include the local community.

Samuel loved to watch her face as she spoke so passionately of all the ideas she had for the park. Veronica got up to go to the ladies and the woman he saw earlier passed his table and went out of the door. As she passed his table, he noticed something had floated from her handbag. He went to retrieve it and give it back to her but when he looked up at the door, she had disappeared. He glanced at the picture in his hand of a young girl asleep, holding a baby and his heart nearly stopped as he realised what he was holding and suddenly so many things in his life and head clicked into place. He slid the photograph into his pocket and said nothing to Veronica when she returned to her seat, but she sensed his unrest and they cut their lunch short. He went home to work things out in his head and do some private investigating to see if his suspicions were correct.

As Veronica left the restaurant, she felt that Samuel had suddenly gone very quiet over their lunch and she wondered what had changed his mood but when she'd asked him, he'd just shrugged and passed it off. Maybe it was work, she thought.

CHAPTER THIRTEEN

Veronica had been busy trying to contact the council who ran Glen Howe Park to arrange a meeting of what she hoped would give her the go ahead to implement her ideas. She'd rang them several times and was unable to find anyone who was able to commit to a meeting. She'd emailed, sent letters and was waiting, but no replies came through. She was getting very frustrated at how long things were taking to arrange a meeting, she knew she lacked patience as she was often told but felt that you could be too patient and it didn't get you anywhere. She called the number at the council offices again and was put through to someone called Rupert Wright who said he would meet her in the council offices the following Friday at 2pm. Great, she thought at last and started making notes of all the ideas she had for the park.

Veronica didn't know where the money would come from as her resources had run a little dry, so she had decided to sell her apartment to release some equity and then buy something cheaper. She knew her apartment had gained a lot of value since she had bought it and the area had really grown, becoming a vibrant 'yuppie' area with new wine bars, restaurants and galleries; making it a great place to live. She loved her home but would also love to start afresh and create a new home and a source of income. It made her happy creating a new vision and watching it develop; a bit like having a baby and watching it grow, not that she'd been able to watch her baby in the real sense of the word.

Veronica was a little early and waiting in the reception at the council office when a tall, smiling man came through to meet her and said he was Rupert Wright. He shook her hand and asked her to follow him through to his office. As she sat down across from his desk in the council offices, she was rather surprised when she saw him, not at all what she expected from a council office clerk, gathering that he was Head of the Amenities Department in the whole of South Yorkshire. He was very athletic looking, tall and fair with very twinkly eyes behind his dark, rimmed glasses which gave him an intelligent look. He asked if she would like a coffee and she accepted, trying to get him into a more relaxed frame of mind while she told him of her ideas for the park.

She had done a lot of research into grants and loans for the creation and reconstruction of parks and historic houses. She told him how she wanted to change the park area into a working craft and art centre for the local people and for schools and colleges to be involved in. She spoke of how she saw the beautiful castellated house brought back to life and lived in with the tea-room reinstated in the grounds as well as the tennis courts; the huge woodland to be used as an out-wood bound place which corporate companies would use for team building weekends. She expressed how they could reach out to companies which may like to back these activities in the woodland park; and that the huts that Cecil, the old Park Keeper had made could be turned into workshops within the wooded setting. Her closing comment emphasised how it would be a huge creative benefit for the area, bringing fresh jobs and careers to many local people.

Rupert watched Veronica's animated face and listened to what she said so enthusiastically and said he would have a meeting with his colleagues in the council and come back to her with a possible meeting the following week in the park at Glen Howe. Veronica stood and shook Rupert's hand and smiled as he opened the office door as she made her way to her car to drive home. She'd decided that she would ask her cousin, Georgina, to accompany her on the next meeting because she had a very practical way of putting points over and Veronica felt that Georgina would bring more factual points to her artistic ideas. She had been a little worried about Georgina recently, although she hadn't said much, she sensed things weren't quite right at home. Georgina never mentioned

Robin much and Veronica hadn't seen anything of him for over a year, although Georgina spoke of Grace a lot and the three of them had met for drinks when Grace had gone to university in Manchester.

Meanwhile, she was going to find out more about the Arts Grants that she could get if her plans were allowed to go ahead. She felt very excited at the huge prospect of what she could create into so many different spheres and prayed that she would get the go ahead.

CHAPTER FOURTEEN

Samuel was in a quandary what to do about the photograph that he had found in the restaurant. He knew that the sleeping girl with the baby was Veronica and knew the baby was probably hers and wondered if he could possibly be the father. He remembered waking the next morning after the party to an empty bed and a misty remembrance of what had happened. He knew that he had drunk far too much and had been dancing with a delightful, brightly dressed girl and things had gone a bit far, but he carried on with his university course, keeping good friends with Veronica, although now he remembered that she did have a spell away that late summer at her auntie's house. When she returned, they both remained friends and he was seeing Christina and she was seeing someone but that didn't seem to last. They had met up for coffees with other friends and when he married Christina, Veronica came to his wedding with her chap of the moment (none of her men seemed to last). Christina never minded his friendship with Veronica, and in-fact, before Christina left him to 'go off' with her boss at work and she decided that she wanted the largest sum of their house and money, she had encouraged their friendship. He knew why now, but at the time, he thought it very modern and open minded of her. Luckily, they hadn't had any children as Christina wanted to wait until they had all the material things she wanted. He now was in the predicament of wondering how he was going to bring the subject up to Veronica. Would he just give her the photograph? He was still completely confused as to who the woman in the restaurant was, who had dropped the photograph and how she would come to have it.

In his heart of hearts, he hoped that he was the father to the baby, but what on earth happened to it. All sorts of questions chased through his mind with one leading to another. He really was going to have to breach the subject to her and hope it didn't spoil their friendship.

He was meeting Veronica that evening and he had the photograph in his pocket thinking that he would decide over dinner what to do. He didn't want to spoil what they had now. He hadn't gone into detail with Veronica about who he was seeing as there was nothing to say. He saw Imogen as a quirky, intelligent girl whom he enjoyed the company of, but he couldn't put into words why he was keeping her under wraps. He didn't know himself really, so he pushed the thought away.

Veronica came into the bistro where they were meeting, wearing her little red felt hat and velvet collared jacket. She looked like a country lady in an 'arty', colourful way and he smiled to himself as she took her seat. He thought how vibrant and excited she seemed. She started to tell him of her ideas for the park again and her meeting with Rupert and the upcoming meeting next week. Samuel thought it sounded all very good but knew how staid and set with red tape the council could be from dealing in his own business.

The photograph burned a hole in his pocket during their meal and in the end, he decided to take the coward's way out and as she went to the ladies, he slipped the photograph into her handbag. He decided he would ring her later to see what she had to say and give her time to compose herself alone. He kissed her cheek goodbye and said he would speak later. She said "Ok" and they went their own separate ways.

Veronica went into her apartment and took her coat off thinking of Samuel and how he still seemed a little quiet and not quite himself. She wondered why he said he was going to ring later. She opened her bag to get her purse and saw the photograph. Her stomach fell when she saw the picture of herself as a young 17-year-old girl with her baby and she started to shake with shock. She had to sit down and rock herself to stop shaking. She had pushed all thoughts away of the time that she had the baby and never knew of the photograph that her aunt Rosie must have taken while she slept, before she handed over the baby to the authorities for adoption.

That was why Samuel had been so deep in thought and why he was going to ring her this evening for her explanation. She realised that she was going to have to tell him the truth and just hoped that it didn't spoil their friendship. At 8.30pm, the phone rang, and she answered the call. She said "Hi", then Samuel waited while she spilled out all that had happened years ago and how she couldn't think of another way out at the time. She told him how she often wondered where her baby girl had gone. Samuel waited while she had finished speaking and asked, "So am I the father?" and she replied "Yes". He didn't know what to say just then, he was so confused, so he said he needed a little time to think things through before saying goodbye and putting the phone down.

Veronica stared at the phone and sat there for what seemed hours. All her old wounds she thought had been healed had re-opened and now lots of questions were filling her head. She wondered where her baby had gone and how she was doing. She prayed that she was happy. She would be twenty-two now and Veronica was glad in some way that Samuel now knew. She shook herself and stood up to pour herself a drink. She had to start thinking straight because she was meeting Georgina tomorrow at Glen Howe for the meeting with Rupert.

Rupert had rung Veronica and asked if she could meet him at the park the following Monday to go over her ideas. He had spoken with his colleagues and they had thought her ideas held possibilities so she thanked him for getting back to her so promptly and told him she would have Georgina with her to go over their plans. Rupert put the phone down thoughtfully and wondered if Georgina was her business partner. Well, he would soon find out and marked the meeting in his diary.

CHAPTER FIFTEEN

Georgina had agreed to meet Veronica at the park to support her meeting with the council officer called Rupert. She was a little surprised and nervous and wondered why she wanted her to be present. She'd dressed carefully in a smart skirt and jacket to look professional. Looking slim with amazing hair which was a mixture of Rosie's red and blond and came well below her shoulders framing her attractive face with blue eyes and full lips.

As she walked up to the park house where she had arranged to meet Veronica, she noticed how the park had grown into disrepair just as Veronica had described and it saddened her too. She smiled when she saw a large hare running over the packhorse bridge and as she approached the house, she saw a tall good-looking man looking up at the house and scratching his head with a troubled look on his face. She had time to look at him as he had his back to her while she walked up the lane to the house. Veronica hadn't arrived as yet and she wondered whether to say hello to him, questioning whether he was the chap from the council office who Veronica had said they were meeting. She decided to go around the back of the house and have a look around while Veronica arrived. She looked up at the window in the house and was sure she saw someone at the window for a second but when she looked again, there was nothing there, just the copper leaves cascading down over the window. She walked down the slippery, mossy steps to the front of the house and was just on the fourth step when her foot slipped, and she felt herself falling, when a pair of arms suddenly caught her and broke her fall. She was looking up into the most beautiful, blue eyes she had ever seen, although they looked at her crossly. Putting her straight on the ground, Rupert said "You shouldn't be walking around the house, it's out of bounds, as the sign says, and dangerous!" Georgina's heckles were risen by him telling her what she could do and she had to bite her tongue because she didn't want to spoil things for Veronica and her meeting. Just then, Veronica arrived and cheerily said "Hi there, I see you've both met" Rupert looked at Veronica, confused and she said, "This is my cousin, Georgina, that I mentioned was coming to our meeting." He looked a little crest-fallen and shook Georgina's hand and she cheekily said "Pleased to meet you" with a smile.

As they walked around the park, Veronica pointed out all the changes that she would like to put in place to resurrect the grounds and buildings. She told Rupert how she had earmarked a grant she would be able to put in place to implement the changes and how a local lady would run the tearoom and have it as a visitors' centre with brochures of walks and nature trails for school children. She described how the wooden huts that Cecil had made would be reinstated and let out as workshops with courses such as wood turning, art, metal and sculpture works. She wanted the tennis courts to be reinstated and let out to schools and clubs for matches; and that she had been approached by a company to install an Outwood Bound course with rope swings in the trees for corporate events, bringing in great revenue. The gardens would be cut back to uncover the many Rhododendrons and Azaleas which had been hidden and lost over the years in the undergrowth and replanting would be done in certain areas to implement some structure to each area.

Rupert listened carefully to Veronica and admired her passion for the scheme she wanted to undertake, whether he would be able to get the go ahead from Head Office, he doubted as the council liked to keep things simple and didn't have a great history for change. He was rather shaken with the meeting of Georgina and how he had caught her, noticing how light and feminine she seemed but also, surprised at the tiger glint in her eyes as he reprimanded her. He could tell that she had held herself back from the retort which was on her lips and he shook his head to continue listening to Veronica's plans. He'd made the date for the following week to meet and give her his report and hoped Georgina would be there too.

CHAPTER SIXTEEN

Samuel decided to do his homework and try to trace their baby. He knew the area where the baby had been adopted, from Veronica saying her Auntie Rosie had mentioned a small tearoom she had visited and that Veronica wondered if Rosie had known more than she said to save her feelings. Veronica had pushed all thoughts away over the years but when she saw the photograph for the first time, all the memories flooded back and released thoughts of Rosie and her movements which were sometimes secretive. She hadn't understood at the time but now thought it could be attributed to her baby. Samuel travelled to Tideswell and tried to find the small village tearoom, praying it was still there and that someone might know something. Luckily, when he pulled up outside a small tearoom, it was open and when he went inside, a lady seated him in the window seat. He ordered coffee and cake and when it arrived, he asked the lady if she had had the tearoom long. She said it had been her grandmother's café, but she had retired and that she had taken over now. He asked if her grandmother was still around and she said that she still came in once a week and helped in the kitchen with her speciality scones. She would be in tomorrow if he wanted to speak to her so he told her he was looking for someone called Rosie who used to visit years ago, and he would call back the next day. Samuel booked into a small bed and breakfast for the night and tried to think of what he could ask the lady tomorrow that would lead to him finding the reason Rosie came all the way over to the tearoom, thinking that it couldn't be just for the scones.

The next day, Samuel pushed the tearoom door open and sat at the same seat, when a small, sprightly woman came in. She brought him his coffee and asked him what he was trying to find out. Samuel described Rosie as being very 'arty' with long, red hair but, it might have been tied up in a bun. The woman who was called Nora said she did remember Rosie very well as she was such a character and how she always came in on a Thursday. She said that she got on well with the regulars and chatted to a girl called Judith who looked after a baby at the large house at the end of the village, relaying how the mother of the baby had died and how the father had been inconsolable. She said that Judith stopped coming to the tearoom after that and the father had sold the house and moved away. Nora added that the villagers thought the baby might have been Judith's to the husband, but no-one really knew, and it was many years ago.

As Samuel got up to leave, he turned to Nora and said, "By the way, I don't suppose you remember the baby's name?" Nora smiled and said "Of course, such a lovely baby, she was called Imogen." Samuel's heart nearly stopped and as he headed out into the street, he thought to himself, surely it couldn't be the Imogen he had met in the Art Gallery in town and befriended. He had been drawn to her in a strange way, almost like they had met in a past life.

Samuel thanked Nora and left with his heart hammering. He had to find out whether Judith had gone home to Buxton which wasn't too far from where he lived. Now he couldn't wait to get back and do some more research, thinking that he wouldn't say anything yet to Veronica because he didn't want to give her false hopes and he wasn't sure if she wanted to open old wounds either. However, firstly, he had to speak to Imogen and find out what her mother was called.

CHAPTER SEVENTEEN

Robin was in a quandary; he had been checking and rechecking the accounts for the Drama course at the university and nothing he did could make them add up. It was clear that huge sums of money were missing. He had checked all the invoices and had talked to Carl twice, telling him how concerned he was as he was Head of the university's Drama Department. Carl had shrugged it off to begin with, saying Robin must have got it wrong but recently, he had become quite aggressive and hinted that he was going to let slip that he had had a relationship with Robin which would implement him and uncover his sexuality. Robin was beginning to believe that Carl had befriended him at the tennis club, knowing he oversaw accounts for his department. He had been so stupid, he couldn't blame Carl for his sexuality, but he would have left things as they were if he hadn't come onto him and flattering him. He wondered before how he could run such an upbeat car and have so many exotic holidays on his university salary and had put it down to family money or another income. Robin scratched his head and decided what he was going to do. It wouldn't be easy, but there was no other choice.

Georgina was in shock when Robin had come home earlier than he had for months, looking grey and worried, he had sat her down and talked to her, telling her all that had happened and why he had been acting the way he had. He kept saying, "I'm so sorry" over and over and was in such a state that Georgina just couldn't believe what her husband had told her but felt sorry for him when he started to shake and cry. She put her arms around him and cradled him, feeling numb with shock but also surprisingly, relieved in some strange way. She felt closer to him in that moment than she had for years and something shifted inside her. She saw now Robin not as a husband which he hadn't been for so long, but a broken person who needed support and it wasn't her fault. She had been blaming herself for so long and her insecure feelings were replaced with a calmness which was such a relief. She never would have believed that she would feel this way after such news but for now, she took control. Georgina had rung the accounts office to say Robin wouldn't be coming into work for a while and someone else was going to take over his case work. Things were going to change she was at the helm now.

Robin didn't go back to the accounts office. He resigned and embarked on a sports training course which he loved and made him happier than he had been for years. He moved out of the marital home into his own flat and Georgina had helped him throughout and they both seemed much happier for the break, remaining friends and very much there for their daughter, Grace. Grace was rather shocked at the turn of events but after seeing the positive faces of her parents, the thought it was for the best. She hadn't been told about her father's connection to Carl and it was thought that no good was to be done by telling her. Someone else had taken over Robin's job at the university who soon uncovered the depth of Carl's dishonesty and he was instantly suspended and would be lucky not to go to jail. As for Georgina, she couldn't have believed how much happier she would have become after such revelations but that is exactly what she felt.

She confided in Judith over coffee just what had happened and she in-turn was amazed at the change in her friend. She said "I knew you'd been saying something wasn't right, but who would have thought! And you've handled things so well, I wonder if they'll charge Carl over his accounting or lack of it?" Georgina told her all she knew but Grace had never mentioned Carl, so she thought he may have done a disappearing act. Anyhow, that wasn't their concern anymore as Robin had moved on. In fact, they all had. Georgina was looking forward to going back up to the Glen Howe Park for another look around and kept smiling to herself when she thought of Rupert getting cross with her when she was walking around the house, then tripping into his arms. She told Judith about him and her friend smiled and said "Wow, he sounds alright" and wondered if he was married! Georgina replied "Oh, I'm not looking for anyone, it was nice to be noticed after being married for so long, but he made me feel like a woman again." she added with a smile.

CHAPTER EIGHTEEN

Imogen was just on her way back from entering her picture "Four Seasons" into the Fourth Street Gallery competition, and Grace, after much deliberation had entered her original picture of Imogen walking though the leaves and tree archway and called it "Flaming Autumn".

Her picture which captured Imogen's original painting was so different now with Imogen imprinted on, making her almost unrecognisable as all the colours were so red, gold and yellow. She kept it in the basement with a cloth over, feeling somehow that she was taking something from Imogen by using her background; although, if she hadn't taken a photograph of it, it would never have been seen as she had painted over it to create her 'Four Seasons.' They had a week to wait for the competition results, but both prayed one or the other would win.

Imogen had met up with Samuel for a coffee and spot of lunch. He was, she thought a little different in that he seemed to look at her much more and asked her questions about her family and parents. She left the restaurant a little confused but threw the feeling away. Tomorrow the competition results were going to be decided and she and Grace were both excited.

Veronica was trying to put her thoughts and feelings in place as Samuel spoke to her gently, telling her what he had found out. She couldn't think what to do with the information. Rosie must have been happy that Imogen was brought up in a happy family environment and Veronica didn't want to spoil anything for her daughter. She had played no part in her upbringing but felt she was entitled to know but was unsure about it.

She looked back to when she was seventeen and so scared, relying on Rosie to help her through her turmoil. Luckily, Georgina had been away on a course in France on a school trip for the most part of her predicament. She wondered also about that now whether it would have been better to include her but with her going away, it was thought best to keep things less complicated and less people would know. She told Samuel all her thoughts and he understood because he'd been having the same thought whether to tell Imogen or indeed if he had the right to do so. Maybe, tell her adoptive mother first and then decide where to go from there.

Grace and Imogen stood holding hands, looking with mouths open at the winner of the competition. Grace's heart was beating uncontrollably as she stared at the large colourful picture and Imogen couldn't take her eyes away from the mesmerizing picture. Quite a crowd of people had gathered around to see who had won and bent down to read the card which read "Love Rosie".

Grace took Imogen outside after they had looked at their own pictures and she tried to explain to her how she had taken the picture of her in the leaves and put it against her original oil canvas and that was the result. She told her how she felt, and she had left it in the basement. They went back to the flat together, but the picture was gone, who could have entered their picture, it seemed impossible and why was it signed "Love Rosie." Grace's grandmother's name.

Bertie came in while they were both scratching their heads and they told him what had happened. He said "Oh, that was me, the older lady with the long red hair you told me about at your class, who spilt paint on your canvas was outside and wanted to get her picture that she had stored in our basement and asked me to take it for her and not to trouble you. So, I thought you would be glad I'd helped her" he continued "She was very cool looking, I loved her long velvet green and orange skirt which she must have bought on Carnaby Street or somewhere in London."

The girls looked at each other in disbelief and went back to the university to see what was going to be the outcome of this revelation and they were told that the picture had been lodged as a dual entry by Grace and Imogen and they were joint winners, although Imogen didn't know that at the time. Rosie's grandchildren would both have an exhibit in one of the top galleries in London - an expression of their grandmother's art.

Imogen, Grace and Bertie had travelled down to London together to where their winning compositions had been placed in the prestigious gallery for all to view. The opening evening had been very exciting, and champagne and canapes had been abundant as well as much praise for the girls' ethereal autumn scene with Grace's photograph of Imogen intertwined within the richness of its background. They had made a weekend of it and saw a couple of plays that Bertie insisted were a must in the West End.

The picture had been sold for a ridiculous amount of money so Grace and Imogen thought, but were delighted with the well needed money to enable them to proceed with their art. From there on, they received such acclaim that there were commissions for other work which kept them intertwined, deciding which images they would combine in the same mystical way of their original photograph. They decided early on in their business that they would keep their own work running alongside and Grace's love for travel made sure of that as she had disappeared abroad from time to time with her camera, only to return with truly amazing images of her travels. She would turn them into a separate, unique form, calling it 'Colour my World'.

Imogen also carried on with her love of painting and texture on canvas and felt very blessed to be able to make a living from her art. She had seen nothing of Samuel since their last lunch. He had phoned to congratulate her but that was all, plus she was so busy herself since the exhibition that she hardly had the time to go for a coffee. With her current workload, she would have to pace herself and could do with a studio which she and Grace were busy trying to find.

CHAPTER NINETEEN

Judith was rather surprised to find a good-looking man waiting for her at the school gate. He explained that he was a friend of Imogen whom he had taken to a few art exhibitions and thought she was a very talented artist, and she would do well. He said he would like to have a meeting with Judith somewhere and chat about Imogen at her convenience. Judith's heart was beating fast, she wasn't sure what this man, who told her his name was Samuel, a friend of Imogen's, could want to discuss with her. She thought it wasn't a romantic reason and that he was a lot older than her daughter, but possibly, the deep fear she always had hidden, of how she had brought Imogen home to look after as her own at the adopted father's insistence. However, she agreed to meet the following day in the café bistro and talk. She wasn't going to tell her husband, Stephen about it until she knew what it was all about. It might be to do with Imogen's artwork, who knew?

The following day, Judith dressed in casual jeans and a bright top and walked into the café at 12 noon to be met by Samuel, who was already seated. He rose when she went over and ordered coffee for them both. Samuel said "I don't really know how to start saying this, so I'll just say what I think I know" then he went on to explain how he had found the picture of Veronica with a baby and how she had put the baby up for adoption, telling her that he had found out where she had gone, leading to visiting the café and speaking to Nora the café owner, who remembered her and baby Imogen. All Judith's fears had been realised, but as she looked at this kind, handsome face, she stared and quickly realised this could only be Imogen's true biological father – the resemblance was unmistakable. The same brown eyes with a flick of amber, the olive skin and dark, auburn hair. She had only met Georgina's cousin Veronica once briefly, but Imogen didn't resemble her at all - she had taken all her father's genes. Judith had no doubt in her mind that Veronica and Samuel were Imogen's true biological parents and she marvelled at how the turn of events had led to her. She had initially remembered having coffee with Rosie in the small café and now she realised that Rosie must have been Imogen's grandmother that was why she had been so fond of her baby charge.

Now she had the fact of Imogen's true birth parents, what was she to do with this revelation? She exchanged phone numbers and she said that she would be in touch once she had spoken to her husband, Stephen and decided what was the best course of action to take. She did feel a sense of relief in one respect, but she didn't want to make Imogen feel upset or indeed, her other two children to know they weren't full blood siblings, although they had been loved and brought up as exactly that. She prayed that Imogen wouldn't hold it against her and feel resentful because they had such a wonderful relationship that she didn't want to hurt her but couldn't really see any other way.

Judith made an early dinner for her husband, there was only her husband at home for the most part, as all their children had flown the nest with university and jobs, although they were always 'toing and froing' as children do. They had moved from Buxton to a pretty village called Bradfield when the children were quite small, and Stephen had opened his own Estate Agent's business in Sheffield which was doing well. He was an old school, reliable sort of chap and she thought herself very lucky meeting him when she had gone back home to Buxton when Imogen was a baby. He had encouraged her to do her teacher training when they were older, and now she was very happy to do her job at the local school. "This is a surprise" Stephen said as he sat down to his favourite stew and dumplings, then saw the anxious look of his wife's face but she said she wanted to speak to him after dinner, so he tucked in with his hearty appetite. He was a good, gentle husband and they had a very happy marriage. Things had worked out well and the children helped them grow strong together. He had gone along with Judith's wishes to say Imogen was hers although, he shared her fears that Imogen would be taken away if Judith told the authorities that she wasn't the child's mother. He sometimes had a niggle in his brain that perhaps Judith had been the mother after an affair with the adopted father, but he'd pushed that thought away. Judith had always been more than honest with him throughout their marriage.

After dinner, they went into the lounge and Judith passed Stephen a drink and told him all Samuel had told her and what he had found out. "Well, this news seems pretty concrete proof where Imogen's come from" he said but was surprised to feel a little sad as he'd always felt he was Imogen's father in every way and didn't want to feel less of a father by revealing her true biological roots. After much deliberation, they both came to the same conclusion that there was no other course to be taken but to tell her the truth. Stephen shuddered to think how things might have turned out if Samuel and his daughter had struck up a romantic relationship, thinking that often older men were attracted to much younger women and that Imogen would have to be told.

Judith called Imogen and told her to come around at the weekend as they wanted to see her about something important. Imogen asked if she could bring her roommate, Grace, who she had brought previously but her parents said no, not on this occasion. Imogen agreed and put the phone down thinking it was strange. It hadn't been lost on Judith and Stephen, the huge coincidence of Imogen sharing digs with Grace at university, with Grace being Georgina's daughter and so Georgina's cousin, Veronica, who she had been brought up with was Imogen's mother, making them related.

"Hi" Imogen called as she came through the door for the weekend with her overnight bag. Her parents were in the kitchen and after hugging each other, they poured drinks and went to sit in the garden on the patio. "So, what was so important that you wanted to see me on my own this weekend?" Imogen asked with a mouth full of cherry and almond scone which she had brought for her parents as she often did if there were any left after Bertie had demolished them.

Judith looked at Stephen and Imogen saw how solemn she looked and thought "Gosh, I hope she's not ill or something", but when Judith went on to explain how when she was a young girl and the whole turn of events that lead her to bringing Imogen to her hometown and passing her off as her own and why. Imogen stared in disbelief and suddenly she realised why she looked so different to her siblings. Only when Judith explained that it was Samuel who had found out all the events of the past and only just realised that he was her father, she couldn't explain her feelings. She wanted her dad to be her dad not Samuel and her mum to be

Judith not this unknown cousin of her flatmate Grace, called Veronica. She went to her room and laid on her bed to think. Her parents had told her it made no difference whatsoever, saying sorry that they hadn't told her earlier but at the time, it was safest as they didn't want her to be taken away.

She thought of her family and knew she was lucky to have ended up in such a healthy, loving place and she would need time to see how she thought about ever seeing Samuel again. She pictured his face and knew he had told her his father was Italian and his mother Scottish in passing, so she had Italian blood which accounted for her dark colouring. When she went back to university after the weekend, she was a little quiet and Grace and Bertie were concerned about her. Imogen decided there had been enough secrets, so she told her flatmates what she had learned. Grace said, "Well that makes us related if you're Veronica's child" and she went over to give her a hug and said "Well Veronica is very cool and so is Samuel – at least you've found out that you have got good biological parents and not mass murderers!" with a smile to try to lighten Imogen's mood. Imogen smiled and thought she was probably right, but it would take some getting used to.

CHAPTER TWENTY

Veronica had told Georgina immediately about the baby she had given up for adoption all those years ago when Georgina was away in France, knowing that she would find out very soon. Georgina was horrified and hurt that Veronica hadn't confided in her and couldn't believe that her mother, Rosie had also not let her into the secret, but there was nothing she could do or say now. She didn't want Veronica to feel any worse than she must be feeling already with everything being raked up after all these years, but to think that her Grace was sharing a flat with Veronica's Imogen was quite amazing.

Georgina went into her spare back bedroom and pulled a box of photos out of the wardrobe after hearing all Veronica had to say, she decided to look through her mother's old photo box that she kept all these years without taking much notice of them but not wanting to throw them away in-case Grace would like a momentum of her grandma in the future.

She pulled the box out and opened the lid and started sorting through all the old photos. Some very old sepia, others more recent of Veronica and herself holding hands. With only a couple of years in their ages, she could never remember a time that she wasn't with Veronica, although they were cousins, they were brought up as sisters. Veronica's parents' Alice and Oliver were always abroad working on some project or other. It was only when Veronica went to boarding school and she went to mainstream school that they saw less of each other. Not that Georgina wanted to go away to school, she would have hated it, but Veronica seemed happy to go and they had their holidays together. As she carried on looking and reminiscing, she picked up a photo of her mother holding a baby that she guessed was either her or Veronica and then underneath the pictures she found two birth certificates – hers and Veronica's only to her confusion, Veronica had her mother's name on it "Rosie Goodwin" which was odd. Suddenly, things began to slip into place in her mind but what astounded her the most was the father was given as Oliver Hewitt which was Alice's husband. Everything began to fall into place. She carried on looking through her mother's box and found a letter which confirmed her suspicions.

Rosie had gone as a young girl to visit her older sister in South Africa on a holiday and somehow her brother-in-law had seduced the young Rosie and got her pregnant. Alice had never wanted children having chosen a career instead. She was nothing like her 'arty', much younger sister, so had agreed to pay for the baby's upkeep and schooling and pass the baby off as hers while Rosie looked after the baby back in England. Slowly things began to dawn on Georgina, that Veronica was her real sister not her cousin and Grace and Imogen were actual cousins and much closer related than at first thought. With this huge revelation, she went back to Veronica to divulge all the new evidence which was unfolding. Everything seemed to look different in such a short time but really Georgina felt it was a good thing. She had always been close to Veronica even though they were so different. Veronica beamed when she told her and said that she felt better knowing her true parent was Rosie as Rosie had always been there for her. They talked about the photographs of Veronica and Imogen as a baby and how Samuel had found it in the restaurant but just couldn't fathom out who the lady was who had dropped it – it was all very strange.

Veronica was going back up to Glen Howe with an architect to see what could be done with the old castellated building and how much it would take out of the grant money should it be approved by the council. She was still awaiting Rupert's outcome from his council meeting and was praying that she would get the go ahead, although at times, her stomach churned and she hoped that she wasn't taking too much on, but thought how it would change so many lives with all she had planned and all the opportunities for the arts and social activities.

Three days later, she received a call from Georgina saying that she shouldn't be telling her this, but she had heard that someone else was putting an offer in for re-developing the Glen, but incorporating a housing scheme which would mean sawing down many of the trees and clearing huge areas of the park. Georgina couldn't say how she had found this out, but she guessed it was through Rupert as she had been out for a couple of dinners with him but was keeping things very close to her chest. She knew Georgina and Robin were getting a divorce and things were very amicable and Robin was like a new man, looking years younger and fitter than the last time she had seen him. He was embracing his new freedom. He had started a sports course and had been on an Outwood bound course in Scotland, returning with loads of ideas of how he wanted to create a rope course in the woods to start a teambuilding arena there which would be supported by corporate firms for their staff training.

Veronica put the phone down to immediately pick it up again and started to find out exactly what the position and ownership was of the park. It took Veronica the best part of the day to piece the full truth of the park's history together and when she had this, she arranged a meeting the following day with the council to give them her findings. She was quite nervous as she went into the boardroom and sat down with her file of documents that she had printed off from the library's historic data. She cleared her throat and began to relay all the facts she had found which stated that the Glen was bequeathed in full to the people of the local area for their pleasure as a park and wasn't to be sold on for housing. The council were only custodians and were not allowed to sell the area for housing development. She knew that she was improving the site, indeed restoring it to its original purpose and reinstating the facilities which were there many years ago with the tennis court and café but also bringing it up to date with today's modern benefits such as internet and teaching facilities with art workshops and Outwood bound pursuits. Veronica had been speaking for some time and now she paused and asked if there were any questions. She looked at the five council members with their pens poised and scratching away, waiting for their comments. Rupert was the first to speak and said, "Thank you Veronica for your report, if you would give us another day, we will have made our decision and get back to you". She thanked them for listening and left and thought she couldn't do anymore. It was in the lap of the gods now.

The next day at 10am, the phone rang and Rupert's deep voice said, "Well done Veronica, you got the go ahead, congratulations!" She would have kissed him if he had been there. He went on to say that he would have all the paperwork drawn up to sign. As Veronica put the phone down with her heart thumping, she picked up her car keys and drove to Samuel's house, knowing that he worked at home on Tuesday mornings. As she rang his doorbell and he answered it, she didn't have to say anything because he drew her into his arms and hugged her, saying "Well done you!" and pulled her inside and shut the door.

CHAPTER TWENTY-ONE

Veronica came downstairs to the wonderful smell of fresh coffee and warm croissants. Samuel smiled at her as she came into the kitchen and sat down. He walked over, kissed the top of her head and passed her a coffee and croissant. She felt strange as things had changed a lot between with all the new information about Imogen which bound them together and her feelings so jubilant over the park had made things move rather quickly and she had just gone along with the moment. Now she was wondering if she had done the right thing by her staying overnight. They had made love much of the night and she was amazed how well they clicked together as though they had been together forever and were so natural with each other and there was no denying the electricity between them. As she looked at Samuel over her coffee cup, assessing his broad shoulders and athletic legs in his shorts, she was amazed they hadn't come to this much earlier, but she didn't know what was next. Did they go back to the way they were before? She would hate to go forward with him and then lose his friendship and support if things didn't work out. She shook herself and decided to concentrate on the Glen and put all her energy into the huge project she had before her. In her experience, time sorted out most relationships.

Samuel was thinking on similar lines to Veronica. He was used to being a bachelor and had decided not to become involved in a relationship since his divorce but finding that he had a daughter in Imogen with Veronica had really made him revaluate his feelings and found to his amazement he actually loved the knowledge although he had yet to speak to Imogen and didn't assume that she would want any contact with him. She could feel resentment and he hoped that she wouldn't. After last night it would be hard not to want a relationship with Veronica and so decided as Veronica had, to get on with his work. He was away next week with his business so things would be more settled when he returned.

CHAPTER TWENTY-TWO

Six months had passed since Veronica had been given the ok from the council to go ahead and mountains had been moved in no time. The once old derelict castellated house in the centre of the grounds now looking lived in and cared for with a new tearoom running alongside the original house. It was sympathetic with the house and surroundings, blending in with the splendid array of Wisteria covering and the front borders of Lavender, leading customers into the rustic open terrace with benches and seating overlooking the park and all the different activities taking place before them.

Veronica was working with Georgina in the new office they had had built at the rear of the main house. Georgina had really become very involved with the office side of the project and was a marvel at organising the structure of how the website and office should be set up with the help of Christopher who created very professional websites to suit individual businesses such as the Glen Howe Park. Christopher was a colleague of Robin's from when he worked at the university and serviced the university website for them, so he was a natural choice when they were looking for someone with such expertise. He made a wonderful platform for them to work with enabling them to add different courses and activities as a yearly programme. He was very patient and showed Georgina how to manage the bookings, calling in for data updates as and when necessary, which was a major job taken care of in Veronica's mind.

Veronica was looking at all the individual businesses who had taken on one of their studios in the park and there were three original wooden structures which Cecil, the Park Keeper had erected all those years ago when he looked after the Glen. They had all been updated with electricity and Wi-Fi connection and many more buildings were being created which were dotted around the park in the woods with intertwining paths leading from one to the other with lighting along the way in the trees which gave a magical effect in the early evening. As she looked down her list of creative people, she had chosen to lease out one of the studios, she recalled how difficult it had been selecting each person as there had been such a lot of interest in the park and everyone wanted to be a part of its growth and could see the enormous possibilities it would provide.

Firstly, she had chosen Charlotte to run the tearoom. Veronica knew the tearoom would be the main hub of the park for visitors to go in for refreshments and collect information from the visitors' information centre, placed inside, then go out to find all the interesting arts and crafts and activities that the park had to offer. Charlotte was full of ideas and would provide different menus throughout the year to suit the time of year with all locally sourced ingredients. Veronica thought she would have to restrict herself from all the wonderful cakes and creations that Charlotte made, or she would be putting on the pounds. Charlotte had just finished her catering course and was delighted to be able to run the tearoom with the help from Evie and Pam from the village who were happy to be working in such a creative environment.

Imogen and Grace had each taken one of the workshops. Imogen as an art gallery and studio where she would work and Grace much the same with her photography beautifully displayed of her wonderful scenery. She had taken to travelling quite a lot since leaving university and her photography took her far afield capturing pictures of wild animals in their natural environment and were very sought after. She would also run photography courses when she was at the park. Both girls brought a great amount of beauty and diversity to the park and Veronica was grateful for that and also so wonderful to see Imogen in and around the park with her paints and working on her latest pieces. She sometimes found herself watching her daughter walk down the Glen and could pinch herself because she couldn't believe the way things had worked out and was so grateful to Judith for bringing her up to be such a wonderful, happy girl. She still felt guilty for not keeping her but knew the way she felt previously and that she had no choice. She had met up with Judith and had a long talk and she was relieved how well they had both enjoyed putting the pieces of their lives together.

She and Samuel had tried to keep as low a profile as possible with Imogen, not to interfere and make her feel uncomfortable with her new found parentage; and her wanting to have a workshop here in the park was really looking as though their approach was working. Judith was often to be seen with Imogen and popped into the office for a coffee and a catch up, especially with Georgina who had given up her school work and taken up the running of the office full time. Judith didn't get to see much of her anymore, plus any spare time Georgina had was often spent with Rupert now which Veronica was very happy about as Georgina was so bright, cheerful and positive.

Veronica and Samuel had grown very close since his return from his business trip and she often ended up staying over at his house. It was a very good arrangement for them both and she was happy how naturally things had fallen into place.

As she looked again at her list, she saw Molly and Zac, who had the workshop at the top end of the park. They were potters and had installed a kiln and made vases, plates, dishes and all manner of pottery, each piece unique, they intended running workshops alongside selling their products. Places were filling up fast with people booking them online in advance. Molly and Zac were brother and sister and Molly was very strong looking, making huge pots and urns which were of a slipware type of pottery which she coloured and glazed. Zac was much slighter in build and his work was reflected in a more fragile pottery including comical cats, dogs and mice which were very popular. He'd made a Noah's Arch with all the animals inside and leading out which was truly a work of art and had taken him weeks to complete. It was now in pride of place in the workshop window with a hefty price tag on. Veronica half felt that Zac didn't really want to sell it as he had put so much love into it.

Next was Ben who was a very skilled wood turner who was handsome and had a lovely way about him. He would spend hours walking up and down the river which ran through the park collecting unusual pieces of wood that he could craft into some interesting pieces of art. His workshop smelt of all sorts of forest woods: oak, ash and beech, which really lifted the senses upon entering and he had an amazing array of marvellous sculptures of wooden bowls and reworked antique furniture. He also made animals from wicker such as hens and geese and had made a magnificent horse which stood at the door of his wooden workshop. These courses were the most sought after, especially, funnily enough, with the ladies. Veronica smiled to herself. He was a very attractive tutor. The women crafted the animal of their choice and could take it home upon completion. When Veronica popped in to see how everyone was, as she did most days, she was amused to see a spellbound lady asking Ben if her goose looked wonky! She had found Imogen on more than one occasion inside his workshop happily chatting away to him while stroking 'Taxi', his spaniel who was always by his side and she wondered if romance was in the air.

The Flower Barn as Isabelle or 'Issy' as she liked to be called, had called it, was a picture outside as well as inside with an array of potted plants and flowers leading to the doorway and then inside, a riot of colourful flowers which smelt amazing and added a wonderful bonus to the park. Issy was taking wedding orders and flowers for all occasions and had a little yellow sign-written van that she used for her deliveries. She had been busy from the beginning as there wasn't a florist in the surrounding area. Issy was married with two children at school and was delighted to open her flower workshop as she was a florist before the children came along. She had kept her hand in, working at busy times in a Sheffield florist, but was so happy to be working for herself and finding how busy she had become.

Just over the old packhorse bridge which crossed the river and wound its way down the park with two more bridges to cross by, were wooden bridges not as ancient and beautiful as the old packhorse which was constructed of stone, was the Sewing Bee lodge. This was run by Olivia and Matilda, Olivia was an innovative, creative clothes designer and hoped to run a fashion show later in the year with her designs and Matilda also worked with mainly vintage materials, making aprons and pretty throws and covers. She was also a very good rag rug maker. Veronica had ordered one from her after picking the colours she liked and thought it would look good in her apartment. Olivia and Matilda had just finished their degrees and were hoping to use their knowledge of fabric and design to make a living working with quality fabric creating designer pieces.

Veronica had tried to fill the park's enterprises with as much diversity as she could and was delighted when Matt and Robert came along with pieces of stained glass and metalwork which truly showed their skills as artists. Robert was a retired blacksmith but had turned his full-time work into a more creative art form and Matt, his son, complemented his work by adding the stained glass in some aspects of his work. Matt was also kept busy at church window restorations which he had a good reputation for. Robert sculptured the metal he worked with into animals, water features and all manner of unusual shapes. They had already commissioned him to make two pieces for the park, one which was to go in the river at its widest point where you could view as you stood looking down the park from the old bridge. It was of a metal flower which petals opened and closed as the water rose up through its stalk and created a waterfall effect. The second was of a group of three deer which were to be placed under the old oak tree at the top of the glen and would be lit beautifully in the evening from the lights in the branches of the majestic tree. Matt worked with stained glass making lamps and was also commissioned by the park to make a new window in the door of the tearoom depicting the packhorse bridge with the trees and flowing river which he was still working on.

Andrew, the park keeper was busy in the park sawing some branches back, as Veronica made her daily walk around and he waved at her as she was making her way over to the rope course to the west of the park. Robin and his new business partner, Jacob had taken a large plot to make their outdoor activity rope course which included climbing through nets, swinging from ropes and climbing the wooden constructions they had erected. They had aimed this business to the corporate sector for team building, it was an idea that Robin had brought back from a course that he had been on in Scotland and realised there was a huge market for firms who wanted just this sort of activity to boost morale and teamwork among their employees. Robin had met Jacob in Scotland while he was on his course, he was much younger than Robin and very good with group talks and getting the comradery going between each team. Robin and Georgina had remained friends and had both moved on and it was good to see the happiness they had both found.

On her way back down the glen, she chatted to Andrew, praising him on his hard work. He and Linda lived in the Park's house with Andrew tending the gardens and Linda helping in the tearoom when they were baking, making delicious fruit cakes. Andrew had worked with the designers of the craft lodges, copying the original wooden huts that were in the park. Veronica remembered their round shape and they used to be called Bug Huts because of their shape and you could escape from the midges in the woods. Now they were much more elaborate but still had the nostalgic look of the original Bug Huts.

Veronica often thought of her mother, Rosie, as she now knew she was. She likened it to not being able to see music though knowing its reality through the sound, and that past lives continue and manifest by the creativity of present souls intertwined by love. While Veronica was busying herself organising the development up and down at the glen, Bertie had been very busy too, he had been in several plays and was having a very successful time, receiving much accolade in theatres around the country. He had already laid his claim down for a plot in the glen design in the woods where a huge clearing made it the perfect place for his amphitheatre. He had signed a lease for the site and gained an Arts grant to tier the area of grounds for seating and lighting. It was a magical theatre space, and he was so excited about it. His first production there was going to be 'A Midsummer Night's Dream' and he had already cast parts from many of his theatre friends who were just as excited as he was to be in the first production in the amphitheatre. He was calling the theatre 'The Bertram Allcock Theatre School'.

When Veronica saw the sign go up at the entrance of the tree lined walk into its tiered seating, open theatre where trees circulated the outer seating, she smiled at his name, bringing back a sudden memory of Rosie taking herself and Georgina to visit a friend of hers that they called Granny Allcock. She lived in a large house with a lovely garden and was a very smart, tiny lady with long, grey hair that she always kept in a neat bun. Her husband had been a very good violinist. Veronica knew she wasn't her real granny, but she had always been called that and she decided to throw any connection away. There had been quite enough of that to last a lifetime, but it was a good memory. Rosie had so many artsy friends which had enriched their lives and she would be always grateful for that early education of the diversity of the people through their lives and how they all came to enrich future generations without even knowing it.

Bertie had written a couple of short plays he'd made into murder mysteries and his first murder mystery weekend had been a huge success which caused much hilarity. His customers had stayed in a local hotel in Oughtibridge and then met each morning with Bertie to be given their new set of clues which took them through the wood and involved all the craft huts to find the answer to their clues. They all stopped for a delicious lunch in the tearoom where Charlotte played along with their questions.

Bertie disappeared from time to time when he was performing on a play, but his fellow actors kept things going and stood in for him until his return.

CHAPTER TWENTY-THREE

Veronica was having a cup of coffee and a piece of carrot cake in the tearoom, sitting outside on the veranda enjoying the wonderful aromatic coffee that Charlotte bought in from a supplier in Harrogate which was an exceptional continental blend. She looked over at the almost bare trees now the autumn weather had stripped the leaves from their boughs and could see the two fields beyond the park and thought of the times when she and Georgina as young girls used to step along the slippery path through the field to reach their favourite playground, the glen with its many treasures. She remembered an old gentleman they often passed on their walk who was called 'Whistler Revitt' because he was always whistling and was very good at it, a bit like Roger Whittaker used to whistle. He used to say as he passed 'Walk on the top side girls, the water runs to the bottom' as they slipped and slid along the muddy paths, then he'd tip his trilby hat as men used to and went on his way.

Thinking that it was funny how she remembered some things in her life and used the phrase throughout, she'd always tried to keep on the topside ever since in more ways than one. Veronica had come a long way and learned many lessons. She knew life wasn't meant to be about being jolly and happy all the time, it was about caring and loving and hurting and grieving and hoping and dreaming, there was no beginning and no end, just the journey and she knew in her heart the journey was never ending.

CHAPTER TWENTY-FOUR

Bertie was rather worried. He was still trying to cast the part of Demetrius in his 'Mid-Summer Night's Dream' and another worry had turned up the previous day in the form of his old tutor at university, Carl. Bertie knew Carl had left under a cloud, but things had been covered over for the sake of the reputation of the university, but Carl had been unable to work since and he had come asking Bertie for a part in his play to try and get his foot back in the door. Bertie knew nothing of Carl's connection to Robin and had said there may be a role for him as Demetrius. Three weeks passed and Carl had been given the role as Demetrius and he had kept a low profile within the park especially with Georgina. She had been incensed when she found out Bertie had cast Carl in a part but there was nothing she could do as long as he kept out of her way and if he tried any of his dirty tricks again, she'd shoot him down in flames. Robin wasn't too pleased either to find Carl in the park theatre and it rather sullied the overall feeling which wasn't there before.

Bertie still felt anxious over his casting of Carl but he was very good in the role of Demetrius and had been very professional in rehearsals, so he threw his doubts away. Carl had tried to charm Bertie to begin with, but Bertie would have none of it and he felt Carl had some other interest in the park but couldn't put his finger on who it could be, hopefully, he would disappear once the play had run and get another part in some other production further away.

Molly was another person not very happy with the appearance of Carl in the park. He had taken to calling in the pottery barn and trying to charm them which washed over Molly and she was very cool with him. Zac, on the other hand, was enthralled by the tall, handsome new actor who complimented him on his pottery and artwork. They would disappear together for walks in the woods and Molly was left dealing with customers and trying to complete her work. Also, as siblings, they had been very close and Zac had become secretive, sullen and snappy with her when she commented on her dislike of Carl, erupting like a volcano, so she tried not to go there. She tried to find out more about Carl, knowing that Robin didn't like him being there, but he couldn't be drawn as to why, so she asked Jacob, Robin's partner and he seemed not to know anything either. She couldn't understand why he was taking such an interest in Zac, who was so eager to have a friend, he made it easy for Carl to get a foot in the door.

Robin and Jacob were busy checking over all the ropes and climbing frames as they had a group from a bank in town booked in the following day. Robin climbed to the top frame and was on the slip rope that swung across the gorge when all of a sudden, he felt a jerking as the rope snapped and he felt himself falling to the ground, then nothing. Everyone in the park had heard his cries and all ran to the ropes course where they found Jacob kneeling by Robin's side in a terrible state. Robin was unconscious and an ambulance was called and arrived quickly, taking him to hospital. He was still alive and gained consciousness in the ambulance. Once at the hospital, they found that he had a broken leg and concussion, but they said he was very lucky it was autumn as a huge pile of leaves had broken his fall in the gorges and it could have been much worse.

Once it was assessed that Robin was going to be ok, Jacob went back to the glen to inspect the ropes. What he found made him so angry and sick, the rope that Robin had fallen from had been cut and frayed on purpose by someone.

The police were called and everyone in the park was questioned as to their whereabouts between the day before and the time Robin went on the ropes. Everyone said where and who they were with in their statements and Georgina was a little worried as Imogen said she was with Ben in the evening, yet she was sure Grace had said they were having an evening out together.

Ben only had Taxi, his dog for an alibi as he had been for a walk through the woods when he had finished work to see if he could collect any new pieces of wood. He had walked down the river and thrown a stone in for Taxi, as Taxi, although 8 years old, was still as energetic as a puppy, plus it gave him a good walk at the end of the day. He'd passed by the rope course and thought he had heard someone and Taxi had growled, but he didn't see anything. Imogen had surprised him when she said she'd been with him, but he'd gone along with it thinking that it gave her an alibi as well. Carl, when questioned, said he had gone out for dinner with Zac and had spent the evening with him. Molly was upset with the way Zac was behaving because he was so quiet, then suddenly angry and not himself at all. He'd always been so easy going and content with his work and now she was lucky to get a grunt out of him after the incident. Although he'd began to distance himself from Carl and said he was busy when Carl asked if he wanted to meet up which worried Molly and pleased her at the same time. There was just something she didn't trust about Carl and she couldn't put her finger on it.

Meanwhile, Robin was making a good recovery and was back at the ropes with a pot on his leg and a crutch for support. Jacob had kept things going and they had managed not to let the incident get out to spare their business. Robin mainly saw to the bookings and administration side of the course and Matt saw to the physical side of running the course and getting the team to work together. Since the incident, they had been extra diligent and yet Robin wanted to get to the bottom of it. He wondered if another business of the same thing was trying to jeopardise their course. Plus, he wouldn't put it past Carl, he thought, to get back at him for not covering for his deceit at the university.

Zac just couldn't think straight. He had got himself into a tight corner. He had felt so happy when he was with Carl, with his charming praises, dinners out and lovely walks in the woods. Zac had very few friends and was a bit of a loner, not being into football or sport as most guys at his college had been, so was delighted when Carl made a fuss of him. He had been so happy to begin with but then the day before Robin's fall, he had seen Carl walking up in the woods in the evening. Zac had gone back to his workshop late in the evening to fire his kiln up as he had forgotten a customer's order and it needed completing for the following day. When he'd finished, he'd gone up to see if he could see Carl and couldn't, so gave up and went home. He thought it very odd because they'd had dinner together earlier and he'd not mentioned going back up to the woods, in-fact, he'd given Zac as his alibi.

Now he didn't know what to do, he'd heard gossip about Carl having some history with Robin and how they had fallen out, in-fact Molly had tried to put him off Carl from the beginning. He had approached Carl to begin with, hoping he would give him a reason for being in the woods that evening, but when Carl's face had gone dark and angry and he started saying he was wrong and mistaken and imagined it all, Zac knew it must have been Carl who'd cut the ropes. He'd tried to stay out of his way and made sure Molly was with him most of the time. Molly soon picked up on his strange behaviour which worried her. Zac was so frightened of Carl as he'd more or less said that he'd regret if he spilled the beans.

It was early morning and Zac arrived at the workshop and was having difficulty opening the door, when he saw the scene through the broken display window. His beautiful, much loved Noah's Ark, that he had spent days and weeks completing, was smashed and splayed across the workshop floor. Someone had smashed the window and completely crushed all his small animal figures and ark into smithereens. He sat on the outside chair with his head in his hands and that was how Molly later found her young brother. His white, fragile face with tears falling down and a look of sheer fear.

Zac knew it had to be Carl who had done this to keep him from speaking. He'd smashed his most loved and revered piece of work as a threat as to what he would do if he said anything. Molly hugged her brother and helped him clear all the broken pieces up. The only piece which had escaped Carl's treachery was a small lion and she placed it carefully on a shelf. Molly was sure Carl was behind this, but Zac wouldn't or couldn't say anything. However, she was going to sort this Carl out once and for all and get to the bottom of things, this had gone too far. She wanted her little brother back to the happy chap he had been before Carl had entered his life.

Carl was on his way up the glen on the lookout for Bertie to have another talk to him when he spotted Imogen making her way up to Ben's workshop. Just as he got near to her, Taxi, Ben's dog ran out to greet her as she always fussed him, then Taxi spotted him and growling, ran towards him and Carl kicked out viciously at Taxi, booting him and sending him yelping into the workshop. Ben stormed out and grabbed Carl and threw him on the ground, shouting "You ever come near me or my dog again and you'll regret it" then kicked some stones at him and went back inside with Imogen and Taxi. Taxi was fine but rather shaken as was Imogen, she had never seen that side of Ben's personality. She knew he adored his dog and Carl was totally out of order kicking Taxi and Taxi really hated Carl. She thought he may have kicked or hurt him before and that's why he always growled at him. She didn't stay long with Ben who was still seething and carving away on his wood in a very angry manner.

She went back to her workshop and decided to get on with her latest canvas which based on the whole of the layout of the park. She was enjoying painting all the individual wooden lodges with the fairy lights in-between; the tree lined lanes intertwined with each other; the lovely packhorse bridge over the tumbling river with the rope course at the top of her painting area; and the amphitheatre with its tiered seating and circular central stage. She had painted all the park's characters on the seating and 'Bertie' central stage.

Ben rose next morning and shouted Taxi to come get his breakfast, but he just looked from his bed, wagged his tail a bit then put his head back down. Ben was very worried and wondered if Carl's kick had hurt him more than he thought. He had seemed fine all that afternoon, in fact he'd gone his usual tear around the park which he did on his own everyday getting a pat from all the resident artists. Ben wasn't going to risk anything though because Taxi certainly wasn't himself as he always loved his breakfast. Ben scooped him up and took him to the vets. The vet examined Taxi and said he thought he might have food poisoning and gave him something to help him and to make sure he drank plenty of water. Ben was sure Carl was behind Taxi's ailment and was going to find him and see what he had to say.

CHAPTER TWENTY-FIVE

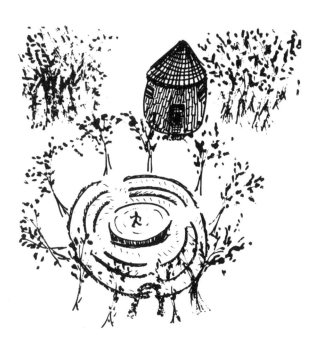

The evening of Bertie's 'Midsummer Night's Dream' performance had arrived, they had sold a lot of extra tickets on the day and Molly had agreed to man the ticket office, selling programmes and tickets. Georgina had also been busy selling tickets as well on the website. Everyone excitedly found their seats in the new amphitheatre, exclaiming about the unusual atmospheric theatre space with the fairylike twinkling, coloured lights which lit all the surrounding trees.

Bertie gave a short welcoming speech to begin with as it was the grand opening of his theatre and then the evening began. No one was in any doubt that Bertie stole the show with his performance of 'Puck', he caused much hilarity in the audience and you could hear the laughter rippling through the woods and down the glen. Carl played his part well, but when the play ended it was Bertie that received a standing ovation.

Bertie's mother was in the front seat and stood proudly applauding with tears in her eyes. Everyone was dispersing and trailing through the twinkling lights, making their way through the leafy woods, back to their cars, chatting and laughing as they went. The evening had been a huge success and everyone was in high spirits, looking forward to future performances. Bertie linked his mother's arm and walked her to her friend's car and kissed her cheek and waved her goodbye. She had been one of the last to leave as the cast and family had poured into the tearoom for an after performance celebratory drink. As Bertie walked to his car, he looked up the glen and thought he saw someone walking up through the trees, but it was very dark and he couldn't be sure.

Now Bertie had time to reflect his thoughts, they turned to Carl. He had been badgering him for another part in his next production and wanted to be enrolled as a permanent staff actor which Bertie had no intention of doing. He had regretted giving Carl the part, even though he couldn't fault his performance, he just didn't fit in with his cast and caused friction wherever he went. He'd seen the way he had gone after Molly's young brother and how Molly resented him, but his biggest fear now was what Carl had said to him after the performance. He'd implied that he would tell his mother about Bertie's sexual preference and that he had pictures of the short time they had together at university. He thought back to how he looked up to Carl as his Drama coach, who was in such a position of authority and how flattered he was when he had taken him out to the theatre. Things had gone a bit further one evening after more drinks than he was used to, he couldn't recall any photographs being taken, but couldn't be sure and he certainly didn't want his mother to find out about that side of him from Carl. He had decided what he had to do now and must act quickly. He decided to meet Carl and put things straight.

Carl crept along the old packhorse bridge, he had been waiting ages for everyone to disperse after the performance and go home and it was pitch black. As he made his way back to the amphitheatre box office, an owl flew by him which made him jump. He shook himself and carried on, carrying a crowbar, he had beard Bertie telling

Molly earlier to lock the night's ticket money in the box office until morning and thought it a stroke of luck to overhear that. When he reached the office, he prized the door open with his crowbar and there was the money box. He quickly grabbed it and went back up the wood to the old oak tree. He had decided he was going to hide the money there until the coast was clear and get it at a later date. He couldn't resist a look to see how much was in the tin and soon prized it open with the help from the bar. As he opened the tin, he heard the owl screech by but then a rustling sound of leaves made him turn, then 'Crack' and he heard no more. The shadow looked over the body and disappeared back into the woods.

Next morning, Bertie went around to the ticket office to collect the money from the evening's performance. He had told Molly to put the money in the cash box and lock the door so he could collect it in the morning. He walked up to the ground's ticket office and found to his dismay, the door open and no sign of the box. With his heart pumping rapidly, he ran down to Molly's workshop, praying that she'd taken it back with her for safety. He'd been such a fool telling her to leave it there while morning but was so sure it would be safe and by the time they all poured out of the tearooms, he'd just driven home. Now, as he explained to Molly and saw the expression on her face, he feared the worst. The night's takings were gone!

Luckily, most people had purchased their tickets before the evening, but even so, it was quite a loss. He would probably have to stand the loss as he doubted his insurance could cover him leaving the money overnight. Who could do such a thing? It left a bad taste in his and the other park members' mouths.

Andrew was clearing the leaves of the packhorse bridge early next morning to stop it from being too slippery to walk over, when he stopped to admire the view from the top of the bridge as he often did. He noticed Ben going quickly into his workshop and also walking back down the glen was Molly. That's funny he thought, he usually had the glen to himself at this time in the morning. He felt so lucky to have secured the job as Park Keeper here in the Glen. He had walked for years in the steelworks and hated it. He had always been brought up to garden as his father was a Landscape Gardener, but he had gone into the steelworks as it was deemed a good, long-term job when he'd left school, now with most of the steelworks closed, the silver lining for him had ben securing the gardening job which came with the house and a lifestyle he had always craved. His wife, Linda had taken to the change much better than he thought she would, making plenty of friends in the park with all the activities which took place. She helped out in the tearoom with the baking and when they had booked parties to cater for.

He had enjoyed the evening performance with
Linda in the park, but he did wonder if Carl would
stay around afterwards. He noticed discontent
between him with others in the park which didn't
sit well. Andrew didn't miss much but kept his own

council and said little. Now as he looked over the bridge at the river winding its way down the glen and the wonderful iron sculptures of the deer that Robert had been commissioned to create which took pride of place beneath the old oak tree. He frowned as he could see a shape beneath them and went over to get a better look. Soon realising that it was a figure partly covered by leaves, he knelt to see who it was. His heart jumped a beat and he stood back with shock as he saw Carl's inert body staring back at him with the cash box from the evening performance by his sides and money covering the ground.

Bertie was the first to arrive at the scene, then Ben and Molly ran over. Everyone was lost for words as the police were called and they stood by the bridge while the ambulance came and took Carl's body away. The ambulance men pronounced him dead and said he looked as though he had a broken neck. It seemed Carl had hidden the cash box in the oak tree and had slipped and fallen, retreating it in the dark, and in falling, had broken his neck. As the ambulance drove away, no one saw the figure going through the woods, silently leaning on a crutch. The park had to close for a couple of days as everyone gave their statements. No one was particularly upset about Carl's death as there were plenty of people in the park he had upset. Ben had just given his statement when Charlotte came up to him and asked how Taxi was because he'd stolen a full link of sausages and a chocolate cake. Ben suddenly realised why Taxi had been so sick and it all added up, so it wasn't Carl poisoning Taxi! He felt quite guilty at the thought and told Charlotte that he would keep a better eye on Taxi in the future.

After a week or so, things began to settle down and no one was arrested for Carl's death. It was left as a mystery, but it did seem as though he must have fallen from the tree. Quite a few people in the park had their suspicions. Bertie met with his mother for lunch and tried to tell her in the best way that he could, how he had always felt regarding the opposite sex. His mother had interrupted him and patted his hand and said "No need to say anything Bertie, don't you think I've always known?" she went on to say "I couldn't be more proud of you and wouldn't have you any other way, but choose your partner carefully and make sure that he loves you, that's all a mother could want" He felt such relief and wished he had had this conversation years before, it lifted a huge weight off his mind.

CHAPTER TWENTY-SIX

Imogen was trying to work out in her mind how her relationship was going with Ben. Grace kept on asking her if they were an item or not as they spent quite a bit of time together and did get on very well. In truth, things hadn't progressed very much and she was beginning to doubt that Ben had any feelings for her other than a young girl whom he liked for company. She knew he was quite a bit older than her and he kept his past life pretty much to himself. She knew he had been to boarding school and Aberdeen University where he studied Geology and that he was from an old aristocratic family from Derbyshire, but his personality was pretty closed on anything personal. It was all about the here and now. She felt that he might have been hurt in the past and all manner of things to try and understand him better. Maybe it was just her ego being hurt with his lack of interest as she had had plenty of affairs in university, but always wanted that something a bit special and different. Well, she certainly had that now, but it wasn't she knew, enough.

Grace decided to play cupid and give Imogen a little help, so she arranged an outing with her boyfriend, James to bring his friend, Hamish along to meet Imogen on an evening out. Grace had met Hamish a few times when she was out with James and he was a 'Happy-go-lucky' chap.

Imogen reluctantly agreed, after all she thought Ben had no call on her to be tied to him when he wasn't taking any romantic interest in her. He'd held her hand a few times as they walked through the glen, but things had to move on, or she'd be an 'Old Maid' before she'd shaken him up enough to make a move. She met with Hamish and they all went out for dinner. She did have a lovely evening and found him good company, but couldn't for the life of her want him for anything but a friend, but agreed to meet him from time to time. When Hamish turned up at her studio to see her artwork and where she worked, it was a surprise for Ben to see her chatting with Hamish and she couldn't help flirting with him a bit for effect.

Ben stared down the park at Imogen. She seemed very animated and kept touching this guy's sleeve and laughing up at him. He'd heard Grace talking about Imogen going out with this guy and he'd felt quite depressed with the way things had turned out. He knew it was his fault, but Imogen was so much younger than him and he couldn't see him being able to give her the commitment a girl like her would need. He had been a bachelor for so long and quite enjoyed the attention that women gave him without him having to get involved. He'd never had to make an effort as with his good looks and charm, women just seemed to be there. It wasn't something he really felt he needed and when he saw other chaps he knew getting married and settling down with children, he felt it wasn't for him. He was free from the worry of family life which came from his own upbringing where he was sent to boarding school from a very young age and raised mainly by a nanny in the holidays. He knew all that but wondered if he had let something special slip away now.

CHAPTER TWENTY-SEVEN

Olivia had finally finished her collection. She had designed twelve pieces and was going to have a fashion parade in the amphitheatre. She was very excited and pleased with her results, having worked very hard to find the right materials and working with them to create her clothes to suit a variety of ages from teenage to middle-age.

Grace, Imogen, Molly and Georgina were all going to model her clothes. They would wear three pieces each and had practiced walking down the amphitheatre steps and on to the circular stage, around, and then through a curtain, back to the dressing room where they had a quick change into their next outfit. Bertie would escort the girls in and out in between, relishing every minute.

Olivia had made half of the designs 'evening wear', mixing an Applique design with a bias cut and for the rest, 'everyday wear' of tunic dresses and casual tops and trouser suits. The day of the fashion show arrived and the amphitheatre was cloaked in a backdrop of blue sheathes of silky material which fell like waves from the trees surrounding the stage and with clever lighting, the colour of the material changed to suit Olivia's creations as they were paraded around the circular centre stage. They had attracted visitors from quite a wide area as Georgina had advertised on a fashion website about the forthcoming show.

The music started up with James Bond's 'Gold Finger' and first down the stairway was Molly, with gold lights lighting the backdrop. Her dress was a beautiful floor length, blue applique design which she wore with very glamourous long, Emerald earrings as accessories and matching wedge shoes.

Next was Grace, she strode down the steps in a very confident, professional manner, wearing a white trouser suit with three quarter trousers and plunging black top which she complimented with black chunky boots and her beautiful blonde hair tied up with black lace ribbon. Grace sashayed around the stage to 'Hey Big Spender' by Shirley Bassey, then danced off the stage with Bertie twirling her around.

As Georgina's music 'Lady in Red' began, she started walking down the steps feeling nervous. She hadn't wanted to be involved to begin with, but Olivia had really wanted her to and Rupert had said why not, telling her she had a very good figure and that Grace was also doing it, so she took a big breath and made her way towards the steps feeling rather shaky. Her dress, she thought was the nicest of the collection, it was a red three-quarter length dress which fitted her small waist then flowed slightly to her calves. The material was a raw silk with an Applique on the bodice and tiny beads on the thin shoulder straps and she wore matching red shoes. Bertie saw that Georgina was a little unsure and ran up to the step to escort her down, then they did a twirl together around the centre stage which looked very rehearsed and the audience gave a round of applause. It actually showed the dress off beautifully, dancing with Bertie and as he twirled her around, she saw Rupert smiling away in the audience with pride. She swept behind the curtain, her heart beating wildly and so relieved, she quickly changed into her next outfit.

As the girls were showing the collection, Olivia gave her commentary on each piece with flourish and style. Imogen was the last to show their evening outfit as the music began, a Celtic fairy forest tune, Imogen floated down the steps in an Emerald and sage green, organza layered, ethereal dress which floated to the floor and she wore her dark hair tumbling down her back. Her shoes were silk pumps in sage green and she moved around the centre stage in a fairy sort of dance and skipped off through the curtain.

Everyone applauded and the rest of the evening went very well to Olivia's relief and delight. Afterwards, everyone complimented her on the evening and she soon had more orders than she had ever envisaged. She really would have to up her game now and hire help to manage her customers' demands.

CHAPTER TWENTY-EIGHT

Veronica was going through a happy phase in her life. She was delighted with how well the park had grown in so many ways and Olivia's fashion show; and Bertie's play, had brought a diverse number of people to the park for the first time. Also, having Samuel to turn to for support was lovely. He had a good business head and always told her how he saw it. He'd got on well in life by being single-minded and it was very comforting to be able to turn to someone for opinions who'd discuss with knowledge, all her different options and choices, especially when developing such a huge venture with the park. Rupert and Georgina had been a big help too with Georgina's administration qualities and Rupert's know-how on council matters. The last few months had been wonderful to have a loving partner too, although they kept their own homes, she loved snuggling up with him of an evening like a couple of love birds. So, when Samuel told her that he had some news to tell her which wasn't too good, she couldn't imagine what he would tell her. She couldn't believe it when he told her he'd been to the hospital and had to go for some results and asked if she would go with him for support. She looked at her tall, charismatic, handsome man with the most beautiful dark eyes who looked so fit and healthy and said of course she would go with him. She had never in her life seen him so unsure or frightened, although he tried to hide it. She couldn't count the amount of times he had been there for her over the years. The times she had been unsure which way to go, he'd give her a nudge in the small of her back and say, "On you Go" He'd said this to her when she was nervous over meeting Imogen for the first time when Imogen had decided she wanted to meet up with her birth mother. She'd remembered being so unsure as to how to explain giving her away as a baby, when Samuel said, "You'll find the words darling" in his beautiful monotone, soft, Scottish accent, then "On you Go!"

The day of the hospital visit arrived and they went in together to see the doctor for the results. What seemed like a lifetime later, found them sat outside the hospital in the car holding hands in such shock and despair they couldn't speak. They just sat there for what seemed forever and then Samuel started the car and drove home.

Veronica left Georgina in charge of the park with Rupert's help for the next few months while she spent every moment with Samuel. He moved into her apartment while she watched and nursed him and made sure he wasn't in pain, ensuring that every day she found something to do with him. On the day Samuel passed, he awoke in the morning and Veronica sat by his bedside holding his dear hands. She had loved him so much for so long. He turned and looked at her and a ray of light shone from his eyes into hers, then he turned to look through the window. Veronica gulped and felt such utopia and warmth and said, "I love you Sam", he looked again into her eyes and again the same bright beam of light shone from his eyes and he was gone. She had prayed for a miracle for Sam and in that moment, she knew he had been given one because it was his time to go. His passing was as beautiful as it was possible to be, nothing short of a miracle. She was grateful for that, as her tears fell.

A couple of weeks after Sam's passing, a large parcel arrived for her. She was most surprised when she opened the card and found it was from Samuel. He'd bought it as a farewell gift. She carefully opened the package and found to her delight, the picture of her daughter from the exhibition which was signed 'Love Rosie'.

CHAPTER TWENTY-NINE

Veronica took back to the running of the park and threw herself into all its many daily duties with the help and support from all her friends in the park, she was so lucky to be involved with. She picked up the pieces of her life and was so grateful for the precious time she'd had with Samuel, although it was months before, she didn't cry herself to sleep. She'd lay in bed at night and go back on all the events which led to them finding out where Imogen was. They never could account for Samuel finding the photograph of her and Imogen in the restaurant. It would be just one of those things, call it magic or not that they would be unable to account for, but so glad it had brought them together.

Veronica had just been to visit Molly and Zac to ask if Zac would be able to make a set of figures of all the people who had workshops in the park, in fact of everyone involved. She'd already asked Ben to make copies of the wooden circular workshops and wanted a large-scale construction of the park's layout which involved all the artists in some way. She wanted the model under glass at the entrance to the park for visitors to see the full scale of the park's amenities at a glance with all the characters in-situ in their retrospective workplaces, working on their arts. She would of course have leaflets and copies of the course printed for them to walk around the woods with. After Samuel's passing, she had needed a new project to look forward to and Zac had been delighted to be asked and said he would start straight away, setting aside a part of every day to create the small figures. He hadn't really got over Carl's vicious attack of his Ark and it gave him a purpose to eradicate the bad feeling.

Charlotte tied her apron around her curvy waist, she was quite small and had brown, wavy hair tied back now with a clip which framed her natural, pretty face. She was loving the hustle and bustle of the tearoom with the many characters who called in. She started work really early in the morning, preparing the fresh scones which were becoming quite famous. She had taken Imogen's recipe for the cherry and almond ones and also made a walnut and ginger alongside which made the tearoom smell enticingly delicious. Today, she had just finished getting the bacon and sausages ready for her steady flow of early morning customers. She already had her orders ready for the park occupants, making a gluten free menu alongside her main menu, as Grace and Zac and Matt were all gluten free. As she sorted her orders out, she looked up and her heart fluttered as Matt came through the door with a big grin, shouting "Morning!" She had grown quite attracted to Matt with his large amiable, personality. She'd heard he was seeing someone, but it certainly picked her day up when he came in chatting to her. She gave him his morning bacon and egg bap and coffee and he sat and chatted while she got on with her work. From the large window of the tearoom, she could see right out over the park, all the comings and goings and felt she had the best view of all. She had heard it was Matt's birthday the following Thursday and she was going to make him a surprise birthday cake for when he came in at lunchtime. 'The way to a man's heart' she thought as she smiled to herself. Matt smiled over at her thinking how pretty she looked with her pink cheeks and flowery apron and she sure did make a great bacon bap!

CHAPTER THIRTY

Taxi was in love, he had fallen for Coco, a red
Labrador which Grace had turned up with one day.
Her friend couldn't keep her as she had to work
abroad and begged Grace to have her as she knew

she adored animals. Grace didn't need much persuading and when Ben said he would look after her when she was travelling, that decided it. The two dogs could be seen every day running in the woods and splashing their way up and down the river that ran through the park. In fact, Ben felt a little neglected because Taxi was usually always at his side but now his love interest was a huge distraction. Taxi had taken Coco around the park, showing her where the best treats could be begged, especially, in the tearoom. Charlotte was surprised when she opened the tearoom door one morning to find not one pair of begging eyes, but two! She never could ignore them and gave them both a morning sausage. Ben had to go around everyone and ask them not to feed them as Taxi was getting fat.

Ben had finished making the models of the individual wooden workshop which had taken up quite a lot of his time as each one was crafted individually to suit the occupants' art requirements, but all were round in shape apart from the tearoom. He was very pleased with his finished results. Zac had also completed his figurines of the occupants and the whole model had been encased in glass, crafted by Matt and now placed at the entrance of the park for all to view. Molly had even crafted a small packhorse bridge and made from clay, a model of the house with the castellated roof which was a good landmark of the park's plan. She had to make several of the castellated roofs because the intricate roof had kept blowing in the kiln, but she eventually managed with a complete building and was very happy with the results. Imogen had painted the background and everyone was delighted. Zac had had to make extra models of Taxi and Rosie as many of the visitors wanted to buy a small model of the park's dogs.

Veronica was pleased that everyone had worked so hard and things were coming together, although every day was a new challenge with so many personalities and visitors booked for such diverse classes but Georgina managed the booking well and worked through the daily schedules in her efficient manner. Charlotte was a little nervous on the day of Matt's birthday. She had made a gluten-free, double chocolate cake with fresh cream and had put a candle in the middle. He had dropped by in the morning, but she was so busy serving and didn't have time for their usual morning chat. Anyhow, she could see him making his way up the tearoom steps at lunchtime and as he entered, she sang over to him "Happy Birthday" and went around the counter with his birthday cake with the candle lit and said, "Make a wish and blow" Matt was so surprised and went along with Charlotte, gently blowing the candle out while looking at her cheery, smiling face with twinkling eyes. He hadn't got the heart to tell her that his birthday was a month ago!

CHAPTER THIRTY-ONE

Grace had just returned from her travels and had collected Coco, her Labrador from Ben. Coco had made a big fuss of her, licking and jumping up at her excitedly even though she'd only been gone a week. When she'd settled down, she walked down to visit Imogen in her workshop. She had seen Imogen had her light on and was busy working on a new canvas. She wondered how things were going with Hamish and Ben. She had met someone herself on the flight out to Italy who she wanted to tell Imogen about. He was an Environmental Lawyer called Alexander and travelled extensively. They chatted the whole way there and had managed to meet up once in-between their busy schedules. Grace had arranged to go over for a photo shoot and needed to travel to Lake Garda and Como and Venice in the week, so her schedule was pretty tight. She had been commissioned to create a calendar on the culture and travel and must visit places for a travel company. Alex, as he liked to be called, had a business client that he had arranged to meet.

They had spent a wonderful day together, where they had walked and lunched by Lake Como. Alex had left in the evening after exchanging phone numbers and Grace was looking forward to seeing him in a couple of weeks' time when he was flying over. Now she was listening to Imogen and how things had not moved on at all with Ben and, if anything, she saw less of him than before. She was going to tell Hamish not to come up to see her in the park anymore as she felt bad leading him on. Imogen was delighted that Grace had met someone although, it was early days and it had been a while since Grace had been remotely interested in anyone seriously.

Hamish was coming to the park for lunch and Imogen was expecting him anytime so Grace said "Bye" and left them to it, hoping Hamish wouldn't be too disappointed. She felt a little guilty as it was her who had arranged their first date. Hamish arrived and Imogen went a walk with him over the packhorse bridge and gently as she could, told him things weren't going anywhere and it was best to finish it. Hamish became quite upset and grabbed her and the next thing she knew he was kissing her passionately on the packhorse bridge in full view of everyone. She was so utterly surprised, she didn't stop him and to be honest with herself, thought he was quite a good kisser, finding it pleasant to be held in someone's arms after so long and wishing Ben would do the same. As she gently pushed Hamish away, she looked over her shoulder and saw Ben glaring angrily towards her before marching back to his studio and slamming the door.

When Hamish had left, Imogen went over to Ben's studio. He was whittling away on a piece of wood outside that he had been working on. He practically ignored her as she said, "Hi", knowing that he'd had seen her with Hamish on the bridge, she pushed him for a reaction saying "So what's wrong with Mr Cool today?" He replied, "I think it rather childish to be kissing in full sight of everyone on the bridge, besides being totally unprofessional!" Imogen was furious and replied "Well at least he knows how to kiss! And he's good at it!" Ben's face went dark and angry and before she could say anything else, he grabbed her and ferociously and hungrily kissed her. She felt her feet leave the ground as he picked her up and banged the workshop door closed. She was on the workshop floor before she knew it with Ben kissing her and pulling off her clothes. Imogen felt as though she was on another planet as he thrust himself into her, making love to her like a wild animal, feeling her senses soar to a crescendo. With both hearts pounding, they were covered in wood chippings and sawdust and Ben raised himself up, looking down at Imogen's beautiful face with her long, dark hair splayed on the workshop floor and smiled at her while picking wood shavings from her hair. She smiled back at him and said cheekily "You'll have to marry me now".

Things moved along very quickly for Imogen and Ben, with them deciding they would like a wedding before Christmas in the amphitheatre and the reception would be held in the tearoom. Isabelle was delighted to be asked to do Imogen's flowers. She was having a natural spray of white Daisies and orange Calendulas with blue Delphiniums. Issy would make all the table decorations in the same theme and Ben was to have a small Sunflower buttonhole as was Stephen, Judith's husband who was giving Imogen away.

Stephen had been delighted when Ben had asked to speak to him and had asked for Imogen's hand in marriage. He was surprised at the sudden turn of events, but he had known for some time how Imogen had felt about Ben and had wondered why she had been seeing Hamish. He loved all his children, but Imogen held a special place in his heart, although she wasn't biologically his daughter, they shared a very strong bond and he felt Ben would make her happy. They were both so in tune with their crafts and complemented each other, he hoped they would grow together and build a strong relationship as he had with Judith.

Veronica was happy with all the romance which seemed to be growing through the park, she looked at the happy smiling face of her daughter, Imogen with Ben and now it seemed that Charlotte must have some magic potion in Matt's birthday cake because since his birthday, they had become inseparable and Grace was talking of someone called Alexander all the time which sounded promising and of course, there was Georgina and Rupert, so the glen was really a special place.

CHAPTER THIRTY-TWO

Ben had been doing some soul searching and he decided he must share some of his past life with Imogen before they were married. She had asked him if he had someone who could be best man and he wished he was having Taxi, but now after speaking with his old school pal 'Archie', he decided that would probably fit in better with Imogen's wedding plans, knowing he should conform on her special day. Archie had been Ben's school pal all through boarding days and his parents had been close to Ben's parents, staying at each other's homes in the holidays. They played tennis, had fishing trips, and would take their dogs on the moors when it was gaming season on the estate.

Ben had arranged to go with Imogen to visit Archie who lived in Derbyshire in a beautiful area near Monsel Dale. His family estate had been passed onto him when he had married a second cousin, which surprised everyone, but it was expected of him and they had a daughter called Sophie. His marriage hadn't lasted long and he now lived alone in his family house with three lively Labradors and a King Charles Cavalier for company. Sophie visited with her nanny once a week and he quite enjoyed his life overseeing the estate farm and his country pursuits. He had kept in vague contact with Ben over the years and was delighted when he said he was thinking of visiting him and introducing him to his fiancé, Imogen.

Ben was driving Imogen up a long winding driveway through some breath-taking scenery and Imogen was very excited about meeting Ben's friend as they turned into a tree-lined driveway where ahead stood a beautiful Edwardian house. As Ben parked the car at the front of the house, the door to the house was opened and out spilled three excited Labradors which raced around their car. Imogen got out of the car gingerly, she had carefully chosen her outfit for the day out and was wearing cream trousers and a green felt jacket. The dogs jumped up at her in greeting and as she tried her best to tactfully shove them off, a man's voice shouted "Boys, down, heel!" to very little effect. They made a huge fuss of Taxi, barking and chasing around the car. Taxi thought it was great fun and raced around and around trying to outrun them. They then decided it was Ben's turn to be slobbered over and greeted, and with relief, Imogen brushed her trousers down and looked at her scuffed ankle boots. Archie came over to Ben and gave him a hearty hug and shook Imogen's hand saying, "Come in, come in, I've been so looking forward to meeting you" So in they all went up the steps to the huge doorway which led into an impressive hallway which was covered with ancestral portraits hung from the walls with a huge fireplace which was ablaze at the far side. All the dogs trotted in behind and Archie said "We'll go to the kitchen, it's the warmest place in the house and to be honest, I spend most of my time there when I'm not working" Imogen was taking in Archie's appearance as he spoke. He was quite unlike Ben with a shock of red hair which curled around his neck and was quite wiry. He was rather slight in build and wore a checked shirt with a mustard tank top and corduroy trousers in a red burgundy colour.

As they entered the kitchen, two of the dogs flopped down by the aga next to a small King Charles Cavalier, who looked up wagging his tail, then walked up to Imogen's chair, cocked his leg to her amazement then went back to his bed. Imogen was so shocked and didn't know what to say, but then the Labrador called Luna, which Imogen thought was an appropriate name for her, especially when she leapt at the kitchen table and cleared what was left off the plate of bacon. Neither Archie nor Ben batted an eyelid and Imogen realised this was an everyday normal occurrence in their household. When she compared her parents' spotlessly clean and tidy suburban house, she smiled at what her mother, Judith would have thought. She hoped Taxi didn't think he was going to have the same manners when they were married.

Well, she'd make sure he didn't she thought. A woman came into the kitchen and said, "Excuse me, I've set your tea in the drawing room if that is alright, or would you prefer it here?" Archie jumped up and said "Frieda, no need, that's wonderful, thank you" Imogen thought to herself that the cleaning would be never-ending in the huge house and hoped Frieda had plenty of help.

As they drove home after Archie had given them a tour of the gardens and stables where he kept his horse 'Applewick', they chatted about their day and Ben was pleased that Archie and Imogen had got on so well. He had asked Archie to be best man and he had accepted delightedly. They had much to catch up on and Ben was very happy to have taken Imogen to meet Archie and hoped to meet up more often in the future. He thought Imogen had enjoyed her day too and Archie had certainly approved of his choice.

Imogen looked at Ben's brown, strong forearms holding the wheel as he drove home and thought how she loved him. He still didn't mention his own family connections, but she thought at least it's a start meeting Archie. It seemed Ben's family estate had been sold years before from what Archie had mentioned, but that was all that was said. She knew he'd been an only child and his parents had died, but that was all. Anyhow, they were almost home and she wanted to get out of her hairy, scuffed clothes, but she had really enjoyed her day.

CHAPTER THIRTY-THREE

Grace was a little nervous as she walked up the glen holding Alexandra's hand. He had arrived the day before and she had told her mother that she would bring him up to her office in the park to introduce him. As she walked up past the craft workshops, she saw all her fellow crafters and friends and they waved and stared as they walked up to the office steps together to see her mother. As she opened the office door, her mother's eyes grew a little large as she took in Grace's new friend with surprise. She looked up to a very tall dark man who looked like a young Sidney Pointer (an actor she knew her mother had loved). He had a very powerful presence and although casually dressed in jeans and shirt, she felt his strong personality. He shook her hand with a firm hand and they talked for a while as he asked her how the park was managed and what her role was in it. She could clearly see the way he looked at Grace and her at him that they were in love and felt happy for them, hoping they would juggle their busy lives to be able to see more of each other. She said, "Are you going up to The Tree Tops to see your father?" Grace replied with a smile that she was and now he would be in for a surprise too. When they'd left the office, the lovely scent of 'Etienne Aigner' aftershave was left behind and she thought sadly of Samuel who was the only other person she knew had used it.

Grace had a good relationship with her father and after the nightmare time they had had with Carl, things had improved with time. She didn't see a lot of him as he was kept busy running his outdoor activity centre with Jacob and she was busy with her life. As she approached his wooden lodge, which was his office, he came out to greet her and gave her a hug, also feeling surprised at Grace's new friend. He was older than he thought he would be and funnily enough Grace hadn't said much about his ethnicity or his age, just the nature of his work and how wonderful he was as an Environmental Lawyer. Alexander had a house in London and a place in Italy which was as much as he knew about him. Now as he took in this huge, well-spoken man who clasped his hand with such a firm handshake, he knew in his heart this man would become a part of Grace's life and probably theirs in some capacity for a long time to come. They talked again for a while and said they were going down to see if they could find Imogen and Ben. Grace had been delighted when Imogen had rung her the day after she had her romantic tumble with Ben and had confided in her what she had said about Hamish's kiss that had sparked Ben to ignite his furious amour.

Robin stared down the park as they walked away holding hands, the contrast so huge, his beautiful daughter with her long fair hair tumbling down her back and her camera thrown over her shoulder as always, against this charismatic, handsome man who Robin could see would be a protector. He would give her stability helping her sometimes flighty, unsure nature that gave her such a wonderful insight into her art in photography. He heard her laughter and watched as Grace threw leaves at Alexander and ran away while he ran after her to get his revenge. He smiled, thinking Alexander would have to keep on his toes with Grace, but he'd do fine.

CHAPTER THIRTY-FOUR

Imogen was busy arranging her wedding. She had asked Grace to be 'Maid of Honour' and Bertie to be 'Man of Honour.' Ben's initial insistence that Taxi was to be his Best Man, as that is what he was to him had given way with Archie now taking his place, but Ben said he would be 'Best Dog' anyway. Bertie and Issy were going to help her with dressing the amphitheatre stage to make the central stage and archway swathed with flowers of heavily scented roses and ivy as the main theme, with swathes of silver and white material covering the seating areas, and green velvet flooring. Olivia and Matilda had managed to find the fabric and the overall look gave the stage a sparkling, Christmassy feel.

Olivia was only too delighted to be asked to make Imogen's wedding dress. Imogen had told her she wanted something out of the ordinary that you couldn't buy in the traditional wedding dress shops and between them, they had come up with a design that Imogen was delighted with and Olivia had sourced some beautiful material to make the dress. Olivia was quite an unconventional dress designer which was why Imogen had chosen her and couldn't wait to see the finished results. Olivia set her other work aside and worked on the dress constantly and when she thought it was time to show Imogen the results and get her final fitting, she called her and just said "It's ready!"

Imogen looked at herself in the mirror with the biggest smile on her face. She was looking back at a forest princess with her long, tumbling, dark hair cascading over a cream and silver shimmering fairy tale dress which fitted her slim figure, then floated in gentle folds of different hues and shades of cream and silver organza and silk which fell to the ground and made it look quite ethereal. She had a lace veil which floated down to the ground which had small rose buds dotted all over. She hugged Olivia in excitement and said, "You're a star, thank you so much, it's better than I could imagine." She was going to have rose buds dotted in her hair as well with the sides curled and tied at the back and wear a small silver tiara. Judith had been overjoyed when Imogen told her of her wedding though she did think Imogen was a little young, but she thought Ben was a good match for her vibrant, arty daughter. She lent her a blue garter to wear on her wedding day and said that takes care of 'Borrowed and Blue', you just need something 'Old and New' now.

Matilda had made all the guests a little satin bag and embroidered Ben and Imogen's initials on everyone, which were to be placed on the table in the tearoom and would contain sugared almonds as was tradition. Matt had made them all exquisite glass tree decorations with the park's castellated house in the centre as a memento with the date on to add to the bags.

Grace had chosen to have a straight floor length dress made in silver and lemon. Bertie had a new suit made in grey and he was going to wear a yellow shirt to match Grace, although, he secretly thought pink would suit him best. He looked in the mirror and thought he looked amazing and kept twirling around which made the girls laugh and join in. Ben said he had some very good suits and was having nothing to do with having a new one, but gave in to the sunflower buttonhole. Taxi was to wear one on his collar too, but he hadn't hold him yet. He thought he would have to take treats to make him keep it on.

Imogen was going to arrive in a coach drawn by a black stallion up through the park to the top where the amphitheatre was and the guests would be waiting. It was decided to have a meal in the tearoom which on reflection, Imogen had begged Charlotte to let her book outside caterers so that she could enjoy the wedding with Matt and not have to worry about the food. Charlotte had given in eventually but insisted on making the wedding cake as her wedding gift to them. She had made a three-tiered cake and told Imogen and Ben that the top tier was to be saved to celebrate the birth of their first child, with a smile and a wink at Ben. Ben pretended to be shocked and said, "Hang on a minute, we're not even married yet!" while shaking his head. Imogen looked surprised and blushed.

Later in the evening, they were all going back up to the theatre where 'Cool and Easy', a dance band was booked to play for the evening. Bertie had known the band and had booked them much to Imogen's delight. She had heard of the band as they had quite a fan base and knew Bertie had pulled a favour to get them to play for them. A couple of days before the wedding, Ben had taken Imogen a walk through the glen. It was a lovely evening and as they stood looking down the glen on the old packhorse bridge, Ben drew a box out of his coat pocket and gave it to Imogen. She looked excitedly up at him in surprise and he said, "Well open it then" and as she opened the tiny clasp on the box, she looked in amazement at the beautiful necklace of tiny sparkling hearts and daisies. She couldn't stop her tears of happiness falling and he kissed them away passionately. When she could breathe, she smiled up at him and said "Now I have my 'Something New!'"

Veronica wanted to see Imogen before the wedding and she went down to her workshop to ask if there was anything she could do to help with the wedding plans. Imogen looked up from her work and thanked her, but everything was in hand. She still didn't quite know how to handle the knowledge of finding out her birth mother was Veronica and as she studied her face when Veronica wasn't looking, she saw no resemblance, yet knew that her reflection had been in Samuel and was glad to have met him before he passed away. Veronica seemed a little unsure and she stayed in the doorway of the workshop she said "I heard you might need 'Something Old' to go with your wedding outfit as the tradition goes and passed her a parcel. She told her to open it when she had gone and disappeared from the doorway. Imogen opened the small parcel carefully and inside was a pouch made of orange and green velvet. She undid the pouch and inside was a silver ring, set with Whitby Jet and a note saying, "With love from Rosie."

CHAPTER THIRTY-FIVE

Veronica was on her daily walk through the bluebell wood and stopped to look down the glen at all the activities taking place before her. It was the day before Imogen's wedding and she could hear 'Some Enchanted Evening' drifting softly through the woods as the wedding band prepared for the wedding party. She felt a flutter in her stomach and put her hand to it and felt happier than she had for so long. She had been for her scan the previous week and her baby, Victoria would be born in June. She had told Sam before he passed and they had chosen the name 'Victoria' if it was a girl. As she looked around alone with her thoughts, she noticed leaves like copper pennies fall from bowed branches, making light their heavy load, waiting for the first silver coating of frost to protect them as they began their winter sleep then awake refreshed anew in the spring and bring forth fresh green arrays of beauty. She smiled as she watched her beautiful daughter, who was so like Samuel walk hand-in-hand with Ben, down the glen, while Taxi ran ahead, and a wave of happiness swept over her. As the breeze rustled the trees, the first snowflakes of winter began to flutter down and sparkle as they landed on her cheek. She smiled and thought it would definitely be a white wedding and from the corner of her eye, she glimpsed an orange and green velvet skirted girl pass over the old packhorse bridge, followed by the hare then disappear into the bluebell woods and heard the trees whisper "On you Go."

EPILOGUE

The beautiful black stallion trotted daintily up the glen with Imogen inside the open carriage. Her stunning wedding dress gently blowing in the breeze. She looked around the fairy tale surroundings she had grown to love and couldn't have felt any happier as the horse's carriage stopped at the entrance to the amphitheatre where all her friends, family and Ben were waiting for her. She waited while Stephen opened the carriage door and helped her down the steps and as she did, she stopped and put her hand to her stomach, feeling a twinge. She smiled and thought 'You'll have to wait a while yet.'

Lightning Source UK Ltd.
Milton Keynes UK
UKHW050419041121
393323UK00001B/27